Brightsuit MacBear

Brightsuit MacBear

by

L. Neil Smith

an imprint of

ARC
MANOR

Rockville, Maryland

Tarikian, TARK Classic Fiction, Arc Manor, Arc Manor Classic Reprints, Phoenix Pick, Phoenix Science Fiction Classics, Phoenix Rider, The Stellar Guild Series, Manor Thrift and logos associated with those imprints are trademarks or registered trademarks of Arc Manor, LLC, Rockville, Maryland. All other trademarks and trademarked names are properties of their respective owners.

This book is presented as is, without any warranties (implied or otherwise) as to the accuracy of the production, text or translation.

ISBN: 978-1-61242-162-9

www.PhoenixPick.com
Great Science Fiction & Fantasy
Free Ebook Every Month

Published by Phoenix Pick
an imprint of Arc Manor
P. O. Box 10339
Rockville, MD 20849-0339
www.ArcManor.com

This book is for

MARGARET L. HAMILTON, THE Wicked Witch of THE North

••◆••

CONTENTS

Chapter I:

Mr. Meep

"I don't understand," the boy protested, "why can't we just spray-paint this chocolate sundae?"

After a morning's practice at the soda fountain, fifteen-year-old Berdan Geanar was sticky to the elbows with four dozen assorted flavors of ice cream and countless gooey toppings. His fingers were cold, cramped around the old-fashioned scoop. Before him on the stainless countertop were the remains of half a hundred failed "experiments."

By now, he almost looked forward to busing tables again after the lunch hour.

"Splay-paint sundae alla same!" His employer growled, peering with critical misgivings at Berdan's latest effort. Hours had dragged by under the restaurant owner's supervision. Berdan hadn't yet figured out what accent the old chimpanzee had chosen this morning.

"Mistah Meep food make by hand! Not make sundae all alike!"

The process which they both called spray-painting was the most common manufacturing method in the far-flung Galactic Confederacy. Berdan's well-worn smartsuit, cut down from adult size, adjusted at the moment to resemble the faded blue denim pattern the boy preferred and streaked below his apron with marshmallow and butterscotch, had been created by this process, along with the few other material possessions he could call his own—everything, of course, but the beaded real leather wallet, which he'd made himself, at camp.

Even the peculiar, supple, shiny clothing Mr. Meep wore beneath his own snow-white apron, over his own smartsuit, had been "spray-painted," which meant it had been assembled from computer memory, one molecule at a time, layer by layer, in special ionic chambers. So had every fixture in the extensive kitchens of this, the "home" branch of the fabulous Meep Family Restaurants.

All around the odd pair, other, even stranger figures bustled about in the bright-lit, spotless working area.

Many were human.

Other chimpanzees, scores of them, were the beloved children, grandchildren, great grandchildren, nieces, nephews, and what-have-you of the prolific Mr. Meep himself. It was, after all, and as its name asserted, a family business.

Not far away, Berdan's friend Bongo Newman-John, a blue-black mountain gorilla in oversized apron and mushroom-shaped hat, was preparing a huge table of salads.

At a counter against one wall, a freenie Berdan didn't know yet, one of the small aliens from Yamaguchi 523, inspected a bank of coffee-making machines.

Gerry Karoh, a short, squat orangutan, and the seven-foot-tall gunjj everyone called "Blue-eyes" (its real name being unpronounceable)—neither of them meat eaters themselves—wrestled a beef carcass from a stasis locker. The gunjj always reminded Berdan of giant sea anemones. If Blue-eyes had thrust its arm-stalks straight upward toward the ceiling, it would have been more like ten feet tall.

At one end of the kitchen, a thick window opened onto a salt-water-filled service area where a *Tursiops truncatus*—a "bottle-nosed" dolphin—supervised a school of squid with electronic controls, busy cleaning the live lobster pens, empty at present, but awaiting a fresh shipment before evening. The squid served as the dolphin's "hands": Berdan could see circuit boxes, each no bigger than a coin and tuned to the mammal's voice, attached to the mantles of the molluscs.

Of all the intelligent species Berdan knew about, those discovered so far—or who'd discovered the Confederacy themselves—in the explored portion of the galaxy, the only ones not represented in Mr. Meep's huge kitchen at the moment were killer whales and lamviin. One *orca* worked on the night shift, the boy knew. The lamviin,

10

most recent of the sapient races to be discovered, were still too few among the frontier planets and giant starships of the Confederacy to be seen often. If half of what he'd heard about their quick intelligence and enthusiasm for space exploration were true, that would be changing soon.

But what mattered—to Mr. Meep, to Berdan, to each occupant of the huge kitchen, and to the paying customers out front—was that everybody here had a unique talent, was good at something different. When someone like Mr. Meep, whose unique talent involved business organization, sorted it all out and put it back together again, as he'd been doing for at least a hundred years, the result was profitable to all participants—and unforgettable to the customers.

This morning Mr. Meep was sorting, and Berdan Geanar, the unfortunate sortee, was resigning himself to the fact that, whatever his unique—but so far undiscovered—talent turned out to consist of, he wasn't going to be a dessert chef. Just as well, the boy thought. His stomach felt queasy and he was sure his face was green. He didn't think he could ever look a scoop of strawberry jujube ice cream square in the maraschino cherry ever again as long as he lived.

Nevertheless, he wouldn't give up without a struggle. "But couldn't we *program* every sundae to be diff—"

"Ha!" Mr. Meep sneered. Folding his arms in front of his chest, he tucked his hands into opposing sleeves. "This rest'lant not serve cabbage patch sundaes!"

Cantonese, thought Berdan with the relief which follows remembering something you've been groping at for hours. Mr. Meep's programmed his wrist synthesizer to simulate a Cantonese accent! Yesterday it had been Armenian, and the day before, Oxford English. It made sense: today's luncheon special was roast duck.

A demented sort of sense.

When chimpanzees had first learned to talk, the boy knew, they'd been taught "Ameslan," a language of hand signs invented for humans who, for one reason or another, couldn't speak. Some time later, the wrist voice synthesizer had been invented, a watch-sized, powerful computer which converted hand-signing motions into sound. Years had passed, synthesizers had improved, and those who used them, human and simian alike, had acquired more and more skill.

11

Now, all Mr. Meep had to do was *think* about making signs (or think about speaking, which for him was the same thing). Microscopic movements in the bone and muscles of his hands and wrists, movements so minute no one could see them, movements even Mr. Meep was no longer aware he made, these were enough to operate the device.

Mr. Meep—rather, his synthesizer—was fluent in several hundred languages, not all of which, by any means, had originated on the planet Earth. Speaking English with different accents—and dressing up in the appropriate costume—seemed to be some sort of a hobby with him, just like running this weird and wonderful chain of restaurants (when he might have retired decades ago) which on one day served Mexican food and on the next day French cuisine.

Berdan had heard that, after hours, Mr. Meep was experimenting with freenie, gunjj, and lamviin recipes. The boy didn't know whether he looked forward to that or not.

Without warning, another voice, a woman's, efficient-sounding and impersonal, filled the boy's mind as if the woman had been standing right behind him.

"Berdan Geanar. Berdan Geanar. You're wanted at home. Berdan Geanar. Berdan Geanar. You're wanted at home. Berdan Geanar. Berdan Geanar. You're wanted—"

No one else had heard it.

They weren't intended to.

Berdan blinked, thinking thoughts which were, for him, the equivalent of picking up a telephone. "Message received."

He thought the words into the near-microscopic electronic implant which had been placed on the surface of his brain before he had been old enough to walk.

The implant, as powerful a computer as the one Mr. Meep wore on his wrist, relayed his reply to the dispatching service.

"Thank you—I think."

For a few moments, standing silent, the ice cream scoop still in his hand, he tried, with his mind, to reach his home number. He didn't get an answer and knew what that meant. It made him angry. He had work he'd promised to do, tables to wait—another personal service the Meep Family Restaurants were famous for—and, despite

12

his embarrassing failure with desserts and the risk of tasting alien food, he liked this job. He needed it and didn't want to lose it.

As the individual who'd summoned him knew perfectly well.

With great reluctance, he rinsed his hands off in the stainless sink, thrust them through the drying membrane hanging over it, and shrugged out of his apron.

He turned to his employer. "I've gotta go home now, Mr. Meep. I'm real sorry. My grandfather's calling me."

Mr. Meep, who knew a good deal more about Berdan's personal problems than the boy realized, nodded permission but said nothing. The Cantonese accent he was using was for fun.

Berdan gathered up the rest of his belongings from where he'd hung them on a peg by the kitchen's rear entrance, and approached the door. Stretched across it was a cleaning curtain, a translucent membrane much like the one hanging above the sink, which would remove the dismal evidence of this morning's sundae-making lessons. It also insured that individuals entering the kitchen didn't bring in anything unwanted—dirt, insects, germs—with them. As he stepped through it into the public corridor beyond, he heard another voice.

"This is the captain speaking. Attention, all personnel. We've achieved stable parking orbit around the planet Majesty. Initial shuttlecraft are boarding and will disembark in twenty-three minutes. Down-broaches will be available after..."

The message went on with details about the landing. This time, everybody had received it on their implants and knew the Confederate starship *Tom Edison Maru* had reached its destination.

Chapter II:

Tom Edison Maru

The world was two miles tall and seven—not quite eight—miles in diameter for young Berdan Geanar, growing up aboard one of the giant starships of the expanding Galactic Confederacy.

Those were the dimensions of the *Tom Edison Maru*, the only world he'd ever known, a gleaming, dome-topped vessel of which Berdan himself, his employer Mr. Meep, and everyone else the boy had ever met, were "residents" or "crew," depending on who was describing the many humans, porpoises, killer whales, chimpanzees, orangutans, and gorillas aboard—not to mention the numerous alien species which those wandering Earth-born races had made their friends.

Inside, just like one of the layer cakes baked in the Meep Family ovens, the ship was divided into level upon level, some no taller, floor to ceiling, than the kitchen he'd just left, others so high vaulted that clouds sometimes formed within them. Rain—even snow on occasion—fell at times like that, over indoor forests and parklands planted by the ship's builders. Birds flew through the brilliant artificial skies, startled by weekend kite fliers or the odd passing hang glider.

If Berdan had thought to look up just now—his eyes, in fact, were on his feet—he might have seen a yellow and red hot air balloon rising in the haze-accentuated distance.

On the lowest of these levels but one, a miniature ocean, dozens of fathoms deep in places ("miniature" being a relative expression), and more than forty square miles in extent, served as living space for the porpoises and killer whales among the ship's inhabitants. Its sandy shores, hot beneath a fusion-powered "sun," were intended for recreation. Its algae provided most of the ship's oxygen.

All in all, when the total area of any of the levels within the huge vessel was added to that of all those levels above it and below it, the *Tom Edison Maru* was larger than many a small nation-state on the human home world, Earth.

None of this was in Berdan's conscious mind as he made his reluctant exit from the restaurant. The essential facts he lived with every day and had been aware of for as long as he could remember. The actual numbers, down to the last ten-thousandth of a cubic inch, were accessible to him whenever he wished, by thinking the thoughts which would command his cerebrocortical implant to provide them.

Implants served other purposes, as well. As he stepped out, Berdan ignored a "headliner," an airborne hologram tempting passersby to tune in various news or entertainment channels with tantalizing hints about what they might see.

Most were full of talk about Majesty. The new planet *Tom Edison Maru* was orbiting appeared to be covered, from pole to pole, with some kind of leafy moss, in some places miles deep. Scientists were fascinated with the planet because, they said, it should have been impossible for one species of plant life to dominate an entire world to the exclusion of all others. Berdan had noticed before how scientists seemed a lot better at explaining why their guesses had gone wrong than at making correct guesses in the first place, a trait they shared in common with investment counsellors and physicians. Just about everything in Berdan's everyday life, from its technology to its politics and economics, had, at one time or another, been declared "impossible" by some expert.

Other channels buzzed with an unusual scandal, a break-in and theft at a scientific museum. Crime was rare in the fleet: instead of being imprisoned where they could learn from professionals, criminal beginners were expected to work, to pay—in a literal sense—for what they'd done. They never came to think of themselves as crooks but as people who'd made a mistake and made up for it. The widespread custom of carrying personal weapons discouraged crime, as well. Thus the media, enjoying a unique opportunity, were playing it for all it was worth.

Berdan, however, had other things to worry about. Compared with other times and places he might have been born, all the misery the human race had seen and suffered during its long, bloody history, it was a wonderful world he lived in. For the moment, however, the boy was blind to the wonder all about him, oblivious, in fact, to just about everything. His thoughts centered on how terrible he felt.

Mr. Meep's back entrance let out into a quiet, somewhat twisted corridor behind the restaurant. On this residential level, few of the streets—most fabricated from a springy synthetic substance, easy on the feet and decorated in bright colors—had been constructed in straight lines. They meandered about, wandering past homes and shops and other restaurants (none, in Berdan's opinion, as good as Mr. Meep's), following leisurely, scenic routes, with the idea of making the journey, whether by foot, by bicycle (a gorilla on a unicycle passed Berdan as he shambled along), or by small car, as important as the destination. Quicker means of transportation existed for those beings in a hurry.

Just as numerous, and meandering, were the many canals provided for the finny folk of the Confederacy. Here and there the color-paved pathways dipped, so people who followed along them could see into the water through thick transparencies set into decorative walls, and so the porpoises and killer whales could see out. And they, too, if they were in a hurry, had quicker means.

The nearest transport patch was a hundred paces away from Mr. Meep's back door.

Transport patches might have seemed like magic to someone from an earlier, simpler age. To Berdan, using one was as common and unromantic as getting on a bus—and amounted to the same thing. People approached what appeared to be a solid, carpeted wall, indicated with an unmistakable red and white bull's-eye pattern, walked right up to it, penetrated it as if it were air or water—the atoms of their bodies mingling with those of the fibrous mat—and disappeared.

Which was what happened, as Berdan watched now without seeing, to the gorilla on the unicycle.

In narrow tunnels miles long, billions, trillions, quadrillions of near-microscopic "smart" fibers, inspired by the cilia which proto-zoan animals use to get around or by the similar hairlike structures which line and clean the human respiratory system, had been engi-neered at the molecular level to ripple like microscopic fingers, pro-pelling their living cargo throughout the starship's many levels. The system would accelerate its passengers away, Berdan knew, whisking them faster than the speed of sound, taking them wherever their implants had requested, long before they could attempt to take a breath, become aware of the stifling darkness, or feel a moment of claustrophobia.

Unaffected by this everyday magic, Berdan passed it by, wanting some time, on the way home, to think. And to be angry. Prompt obe-dience had never come easy to Berdan, any more (if his grandfather was to be believed) than to his father MacDougall. *Bad blood*, the old man was fond of saying, an expression on his face which Mr. Meep reserved for rotten eggs or spoiled milk, bad blood had killed Mac-Dougall, and it would no doubt someday kill Berdan.

Let it, Berdan thought, right now, he didn't give a—

"*Chickensquat!*"

Berdan's unhappy ruminations were interrupted by a rude word he'd heard many times before. He looked up from the yellow, rubbery sidewalk on which he'd kept his eyes as he made his way home, and was surprised. His absentminded footsteps had brought him further than he'd intended, past three transport patches, almost home the hard way, to the center of Deejay Thorens Park. Far across its culti-vated lawns, a brass band played from a whitewashed gazebo.

Unlike the people of many previous civilizations, the beings of the Confederacy tended to honor scientists, inventors, and philosophers, rather than soldiers or politicians, erecting statues, naming parks and streets and starships after them, preferring to single out those who were still alive to enjoy the tribute. Some exceptions disproved the rule: two levels above this, another park had been given the same name the starship itself bore, Thomas Alva Edison.

But this was Thorens Park, and, sure enough, right at the feet of its central feature, a life-sized statue of the galaxy's greatest (and most beautiful) physicist, the woman who'd discovered the principle which drove this vessel between the stars, sat its other central feature, a rumpled study in gray and black, just as he always seemed to be, on a violet-colored park bench.

Old Captain Forsyth. Rumors which had almost grown into legends claimed the old fellow had once been a fearsome warrior of great accomplishment. Now he was in his usual place, silent and immovable as the statue itself, reading an old-fashioned hard-copy newspaper. Even from where he stood, Berdan could read headlines about the museum theft and the new planet, Majesty. He'd often wondered whether the ancient chimpanzee ever went home, or whether he even had a home.

"*Slimy loops of DNA!*
"*Spell 'em out—whaddo they say?*
"*What's in genes won't go away!*
"*Chickensquat—the family way!*"

But, for the moment, Berdan had more immediate problems. Before him, standing in his way and blocking it, he saw a trio of all too familiar-looking faces.

Berdan sighed to himself. He knew what was coming next. What always came next. It made his heart pound in his chest like a hollow drum. He swallowed—so they wouldn't notice how dry his throat had become—and assumed a fed up, weary expression which was affectation only in part. No one knew better than Berdan Geanar how it was possible to be bored and terrified at the same time.

He spoke first. "Okay, jerks, what do you want now?"

"Hey, whaddya know, you guys!" replied one of the three, speaking to his cronies and ignoring Berdan. "Chickensquat here answers to his chickensquat name!"

The particular jerk in question was Olly Kehlson, about the same age as Berdan. Kehlson displayed a kind of belligerent stupidity which bothered Berdan worse than anything else about him, as if he were proud of chanting idiotic doggerel. He and the pair with him, Berdan thought, weren't your ordinary textbook bullies. Olly was a stringbean of a kid, with bleached-looking skin (what showed between his thousands of freckles), curly orange hair sticking out clownlike over his ears, and bulging blue eyes which watered in "outdoor" light.

18

Somewhere, in somebody's battered old attic trunk or a second-hand store, he'd discovered a pair of celluloid-rimmed spectacles, useless in a time and place where correcting poor eyesight was a surgical procedure. He'd pushed the lenses out, wearing the empty, ugly frames perched down at the pointed end of his skinny nose, where he believed—and never hesitated to assert—they made him look "inelleckshual." Berdan thought they made him look even dumber than he was.

In fact, Olly's nickname, wherever he happened to go, was "Geeky." Everybody called him that. He seemed, for some strange reason of his own, to accept it.

The pair either side of Geeky shook with theatrical laughter and began chanting "*Chickensquat! Chickensquat!*" in a way which kept Berdan from answering, just as they intended, even if he'd thought of something clever to say. He gave up, shrugged, and stepped forward, intending to pass between them and be on his way.

"*Hey, Chickensquat!*" Someone grabbed Berdan by the arm.

The complaint—and the grab—came from Kenjon "Crazy" Zovich, in some ways the worst of the three. He was nicknamed (although no one Berdan knew had ever dared say it to his face) not just for his nasty sense of humor, but because he possessed a violent, unpredictable temper (or it possessed him) when other people didn't think his jokes were funny or tried to play jokes on him.

"Hey, Chickensquat, you oughta know by now," Zovich warned him, holding on to Berdan's arm, "we ain't gonna let you off that easy, Chicken-chicken-squat-squat!"

He danced in place around Berdan, turning him as he went.

"We ain't even *close* to through with you!"

Berdan seized the offending hand by the fingertips and peeled it off his arm, giving the boy a gentle but definite shove, out of his path. He tried to walk on.

"Hey!" Zovich shouted at no one and everyone.

"You saw it! He *nishiated* force against me!"

The proper word, of course, was "initiated," and the charge false—stupid, in fact, since Zovich had grabbed Berdan first. However, Berdan realized with a renewal both of weariness and fear, logic wouldn't stop trouble from coming now.

"Youbetcha, Kenjon!" The third boy, Stoney Edders, grinned wide with conspiratorial glee, and Berdan realized the whole thing was a put-up job. This was where they'd been headed all along.

"We saw it! He *nishiated* force!"

Edders' hand dropped to the faceted pommel of the broad-bladed dagger he was wearing. At the same time, Zovich made a gesture, cocking his thumb, pointing his extended index finger at Berdan's head. He dropped the thumb with a flourish of imaginary recoil while making a swishing noise through clenched teeth. It was the sound they'd all made when they were younger, running, hiding, playing interplanetary explorer, a sound they'd heard in every telecom adventure they'd ever watched, the sound of a fusion-powered plasma pistol going off.

Berdan spent a lot of his life dreading moments like this—he'd had to live through a good many—and not just because his grandfather never let him carry a pistol of his own, or even a dagger, to defend himself. Maybe in this instance it was just as well.

Grandfather said it was wrong to inflict injury or take a life for any reason. Berdan thought he agreed: if a Golden Rule applied in the Confederacy (at least aboard *Tom Edison Maru*), it was that nobody had a right to *start* a fight (though sometimes it seemed to Berdan the one way to prevent a fight was to be ready to finish it, regardless of who started it). If that idea, that it was wrong to start a fight, and his grandfather's, that it was always wrong to kill or injure, weren't precise equivalents, Berdan hadn't managed to sort them out yet.

It bothered him from time to time—times like this in particular—how it seemed safe for those who wouldn't obey grandfather's dictum to threaten those who did.

As if they were one being, Geeky Kehlson, Crazy Zovich, and Stoney Edders took a step forward, menacing Berdan.

"*Three on one, boys?*"

The voice had come from nowhere. Berdan glanced aside and couldn't have been more surprised if the statue of Deejay Thorens had spoken. The ancient, immovable Captain Forsyth was on his feet, yards from the bench he'd always seemed rooted to. How he'd accomplished this without attracting attention just deepened the mystery which hung about him like the cloak he now swept off his hip, exposing an enormous old-fashioned projectile pistol belted around his waist.

"You wanna play grown-up games," Forsyth continued in the stunned absence of any reaction from the four boys, "you better be ready to pay grown-up prices."

"Ah…"

A nervous Geeky Kehlson glanced from side to side at his companions who'd each taken a step backward. He imitated them, but not before they'd taken yet another. As they all took a third step, they turned and seemed to vanish from the park.

It was, it seemed to Berdan, a day for miracles. He opened his mouth to speak, to thank the old chimpanzee for his help, but Forsyth held up a palm and shook his head, letting the cape he wore drop back over the handle of his pistol.

"Get yourself some hardware, son. Somebody like me mightn't always be around."

Forsyth turned. Transformed once again (a final miracle for the day, not quite as wonderful as the previous two) into the fragile, elderly being he'd always seemed before, he hobbled back to his bench, picked up his paper, and sat down.

Still wordless, Berdan watched Forsyth for a moment. Breathing deep, he continued along the sidewalk and out of the park. He was careful, this time, to watch for anybody who might be waiting, out of the old warrior's sight, to get even. Pondering the chimpanzee's practical-sounding advice—as opposed to the philosophy his grandfather forced him to follow—he made his way, more rapidly than before (and with more confusion), toward the nearest transport patch.

He walked straight into its tingling embrace.

And disappeared.

Chapter III:

The Dead Past

Berdan emerged, before he was aware of having traveled a quarter mile, from the bull's-eye patch nearest the home he shared with his grandfather, Dalmeon Geanar.

Although they'd lived together for as long as Berdan could remember since the death of the boy's parents, Erissa and MacDougall Bear, in what Geanar always referred to as "a scientific accident," for reasons which seemed to perplex them both at times, the old man and the boy had never gotten along.

Geanar himself almost never left their apartment on the second floor of the modest (some might have said shabby) building across the corner from the transport patch. He was in perfect, vigorous health for his apparent age; but another thing the boy's grandfather didn't believe in was medical rejuvenation which could have made him look and feel like a young man, claiming it was the duty of all individuals, once they got old, to die and get out of the way for the next generation. Meanwhile, he preferred to order what he needed on the telecom.

Compared to most individuals they knew, they were poor, living on the proceeds of modest investments, small shares in the many discoveries and growing fortunes of *Tom Edison Maru*. Yet Berdan's grandfather had always discouraged him from taking a job, in theory for the sake of his education. A few weeks ago the

old man had reversed himself, allowing Berdan to go to work for
Mr. Meep.

Thus Berdan knew he was in serious trouble of some kind—
again—when he saw Geanar, a harsh, preoccupied expression on
his big face as always, standing downstairs just outside the doorway
membrane, hands on his hips, waiting.

"There you are!"

For a brief, comforting moment, Berdan entertained a fantasy: he
saw himself turn around and merge into the patch again, letting the
transport system take him somewhere, anywhere, as long as it wasn't
here. But he knew this would only postpone what was about to happen. He had no place to go and would only have to come back again.
Besides, his grandfather had seen him exit the patch, which, of course,
was what he'd had in mind, waiting for him in the doorway.

"Where've you been?" Geanar's grating voice carried across the
narrow street, little more than a wide sidewalk in this neighborhood.
"You took your sweet time getting here!"

Berdan glanced around, self-conscious. At this hour not much
traffic moved along the street, but one or two passersby had glanced
up at the sound of Geanar's voice. Worse than anything he could
think of, Berdan hated to be hollered at in public—it was embarrassing—but he was helpless to do anything about it. He'd tried talking
to his grandfather about it, only to be told to mind his own business.
At that, he'd been lucky not to have provoked a more violent reaction.

He hurried across the street, hoping the old man would lower his
voice as he came nearer.

"Berdan Geanar, the next time I send for you, you'd bloody well
better not dawdle!"

The last thing Dalmeon Geanar might have been called was in-
conspicuous, even when he wasn't shouting. He was large, with huge
hands and a belly to match hanging over his belt, if he'd been wearing
a belt. He wasn't even wearing pants, but instead, affected a loose-fit-
ting caftan. Berdan had never seen him in a smartsuit, everyday fashion of the most practical kind for a people whose activities might take
them from a hundred fathoms underwater to the bitter vacuum of
outer space; Geanar never went anywhere, and had no need for such
a garment. Geanar's face was broad, red-jowled, rough-complexioned,

the enormous nose in its center almost grotesque, blue-mottled, and covered with a network of fine, broken capillaries. His smallish eyes glittered from beneath a thick, untrained hank of white hair which hung over his forehead.

They weren't the eyes of a kind man.

As Berdan approached, his grandfather reached out with astonishing swiftness and seized the boy by one thin shoulder—the old man's big thumb dug in, painful between the bones—and half-shoved half-dragged his grandson through the apartment building's door membrane, following on the boy's heels. They stopped in the hallway. Geanar's thumb tightened on Berdan's shoulder.

"Now what have you to say for yourself?"

Berdan knew it was a trap. His grandfather wasn't interested, and anything he had to say would be used against him. But he couldn't help trying to defend himself. "I—"

"There's no excuse!" The old man roared down at him, shaking the helpless boy back and forth until his head hurt, until Berdan could no longer control his jaw and bit his tongue.

"Your one business is to do what I say, understand me?"

Berdan said nothing.

"Answer me! What were you up to?"

Having eliminated any possible excuse, why did he now demand one? It was illogical. It was also another trap, Berdan recognized, but one he wouldn't be permitted to avoid, since any alternative was a good deal more painful to contemplate.

"I got stopped in Deejay Thorens Park..." He was astonished that, this time, his grandfather hadn't interrupted him. Hoping against long experience that he'd be allowed to finish for once, he rushed on.

"Geeky Kehlson and Crazy Zovich and Stoney Edders wouldn't let me—"

"Thorens Park?"

Berdan wouldn't have thought it possible, but Geanar's complexion grew even redder. His painful grasp tightened even further on the boy's tender shoulder.

"What were you doing in Thorens Park? There are a dozen patches between Meep's greasy spoon and there! You think I went to all the

24

effort of calling so you could waste your time—and mine—loafing with your no-good friends?"

Only three such patches existed, in fact, and the "effort" in question consisted of thinking about calling him at Mr. Meep's. But pointing this out wouldn't make Berdan's situation any better. (Nor would trying to wriggle loose from Geanar's grasp; he'd tried it before, and knew the hard way.) Appealing to facts and logic never accomplished anything but making the old man madder.

Inside Berdan, an unbearable mixture of anger, pain, and contempt boiled over. "I wasn't loafing, and they're *not* my friends!"

Still holding Berdan's shoulder between a thick forefinger and a thicker thumb, which felt to the boy like titanium clamps, Geanar bent down and peered into his grandson's face. He wasn't shouting anymore. He'd fallen silent. His lips were compressed into a short, straight line. His color had faded in an instant from reddish-purple to white. Berdan knew this was going to be a bad one.

"Defy all precedent and tell your grandfather the truth, you ill-conceived little barbarian." Geanar's roar had diminished to a far more terrifying whisper.

"You've been fighting again, haven't you?"

It was clear to Berdan that, without any evidence or justice, the old man had just convicted him of what was considered in their household the ultimate crime. Geanar wouldn't listen if he tried to deny the charge. Fear of the great knob-knuckled backs of Geanar's huge hands put a quaver in Berdan's voice. "No, Grandfather, I haven't been fighting."

Although, he conceded to himself, he'd have fought Geeky and the rest in an instant, if—thanks to Captain Forsyth's sudden interference—he hadn't avoided it.

"And now you're compounding it with lies and backtalk!"

With a melodramatic gesture of disgust, Geanar thrust the boy away from him. Helpless against the old man's strength, Berdan slammed backward against the corridor wall and hurt his head again. One of the other tenants, old Mrs. Kropotkin it was, poked her curler-covered head out through the membrane of her own apartment door.

"Neighbor"—a warning simmered in her voice—"I'm gonna call Security if you—Dalmeon Geanar, don't you dast glare at me! Just be grateful I don't handle you myself!"

Behind the man, she spied Berdan. Her expression brightened, and with it, her tone, "Howdy there, sonny boy! Always remember: *illegitimates non carborundum!*"

And with this enigmatic parting advice, Mrs. Kropotkin popped back into her apartment.

An embarrassed, wordless moment passed before Berdan's grandfather lifted a thumb. Berdan nodded, issuing mental instructions to his implant which relayed them to the building, and knew his grandfather was doing the same. Under their feet, the section of carpet they were standing on began growing, lifting them both at a gentle pace toward the ceiling. Before their heads could brush it, it retreated around them. They passed through it onto the next floor.

The hall was empty.

As the carpet sealed itself beneath them, they strode to their own apartment, through its membrane—also implant-controlled—and into its small living room. As they entered, a small flurry of motion near one wall at floor level caught Berdan's eye. It was the housemice, out to play when the people were away. In a well-kept modern building, they wouldn't have been seen at all.

Perhaps the humidity slowed them down. This room, the kitchen portion of it, his grandfather's bedroom, and the bathroom were filled with potted plants, hundreds of them, which the old man tended, watered, fertilized, and misted every day. Their apartment looked like a jungle, felt and smelled like one, as well.

Berdan had never understood his grandfather's obsession. He didn't dare so much as touch the old man's plants, as green things seemed to die a horrible death in the presence of what Geanar called his "black thumb." In the boy's opinion, which had never been consulted in this or any other matter, plants belonged outdoors. He preferred animals, although he'd never been allowed to have one, warm things which could move around, with a personality and eyes to look back at you, things which were maybe just a bit unpredictable.

As usual, what could be seen of the apartment's windows through all the greenery had been left adjusted to display the brightest, busiest, most crowded intersection aboard the *Tom Edison Maru*. To anyone unfortunate enough to be without an implant, they'd have appeared to be nothing more than blank sections of the walls. Although Berdan had heard it was considered smart, in certain better-off neighborhoods, to have real windows with real glass looking out onto real streets, he liked these windows better: they could look anywhere.

His grandfather needed the feeling of other people around him, even though he never seemed to like people much. Berdan liked them well enough, he supposed, but preferred to let the windows of his own, one hundred percent plant-free, bedroom give him a computer-enhanced view of the star-brilliant blackness through which *Tom Edison Maru* quartered in her endless journeying. This was another transgression for which the boy caught it on regular occasions. For some reason, looking into the depths of space disturbed the old man.

"What am I to do with you?" Geanar's voice, which had thundered at Berdan downstairs, was now a pitiable whine.

"You're just like your father—and his mother before him! It's bad blood, I tell you! Bad blood! What in the sad, sorry world did I ever do to deserve it?"

Berdan, who knew the signs, began to relax. Grandfather wasn't going to hit him, as he'd feared, but just launch into the millionth repetition of the "bad blood" lecture, though it was pretty serious when his grandmother got dragged in, too. In an odd way, all of Berdan's troubles seemed to revolve about Grandma Lucille, although her tragedy had taken place long before he'd even been born.

Grandfather, it seemed, wasn't the only one in the fleet who believed in bad blood.

"Are you listening to me, young man?"

No, Berdan thought, I'm not listening to you, Grandfather. Neither of them had so much as sat down, but stood not far apart in the center of the overgrown living room. But he gave Geanar a dutiful nod and continued thinking his own thoughts.

Unknown to his grandfather, Berdan had been aware for years—thanks to thoughtful individuals like Geeky Kehlson, Crazy Zovich, and Stoney Edders—that, in common opinion, Dalmeon Geanar carried his own share of the family curse.

In earlier days—contrasted with the housebound existence the old man had pursued all of Berdan's life—Geanar and his wife, Lucille, had been part of a planetary survey, he as a Broach technician, a sort of matter-transmitter installation and repair man, she as the praxeologist whose studies of intelligent life constituted the reason for planetary surveys in the first place.

According to the stories thrust upon Berdan, it had either been bad judgment on Geanar's part or cowardice (hence the name "chickensquat," an affliction, in popular theory, which could be passed on to succeeding generations) which had been responsible for the slow death she'd suffered at the hands (or claws or tentacles) of primitive aliens during the exploration of a new world. This was all the detail the boy had ever been given. His grandfather wouldn't talk about it. Berdan didn't even know what planet had been involved.

"*Pay attention!*" A huge, rough hand landed on Berdan's shoulder and rattled his teeth again. "If you'd stop stargazing and listen for once, you might make something decent of yourself!"

"Yes, Grandfather."

But all the time, the boy was thinking to himself, *Just like you, Grandfather?*

Attempting to escape the public outrage that had followed these events, Dalmeon Geanar had fled his post aboard another great ship of the fleet. Taking his son, Berdan's father, MacDougall, with him, he'd arrived at the *Tom Edison Maru*. The story had traveled with them, however. The son, who according to the stories had gotten along no better with his father than Berdan did now, had published notice of legal separation from his surviving parent.

With all his heart, Berdan wished for some part of MacDougall Bear's courage. He even wondered if some truth mightn't be discovered, lurking in this theory of hereditary cowardice. That his father, according to all accounts, hadn't suffered any such affliction was something he failed to consider, along with a possibility that his grandfather, having learned from a son independent enough to run away, had brought the grandson up fearful and helpless.

In any case, when he hadn't been much older than Berdan, Mac-Dougall had left home, struck out on his own, found work, and began to educate himself. He'd even rejected his father's name, adopting the one his mother had been born with: Bear.

But tragedy is a relentless hunter. Little more than a decade later, MacDougall and his beautiful wife Erissa had come to their own untimely end, repeating family history. Both accomplished scientists, they'd shared busy, productive lives, full of physical and intellectual adventure, leaving less time, perhaps, than they should have allotted their only child.

Berdan had always believed that the facts of his life weren't tragic or even unusual in particular. Those who disagreed with his grandfather about rejuvenation (which was most people) tended to die abrupt deaths, by accident or otherwise. The ancient enemies, old age and disease, had been done away with. Violence was the single real danger remaining, something medical science could do nothing about. The rugged individualists of the Confederacy (which also meant most people), jealous of their privacy and freedom, didn't want it to try.

During their final, fatal experiment, MacDougall and Erissa Bear had entrusted Berdan to the care of an individual whose shortcomings, in their generosity, they'd learned to overlook: MacDougall's father, Dalmeon Geanar.

"*Berdan Geanar!*"

Still standing, his mind murky with remembrance, the boy blinked up at his grandfather.

"Yes, I'm talking to you! Do you think I called you home for the sake of my health?"

Having come to the end of his string of well-worn thoughts about his father and his mother, as he had so many times before, Berdan took a deep breath. "No, Grandfather. Why did you call me?"

Before Geanar could reply, a sudden *ping!* sounded inside both their heads.

Geanar nodded.

The door dilated around the husky forms of a pair of beings, one human, one gorilla, wearing smartsuits whose surfaces had been adjusted to look like workman's overalls.

"In there." Geanar inclined his head, indicating his own bedroom door. The workers entered without the old man and, seconds later, emerged into the jungle of the living room, straining beneath a large, upright crate Berdan had never seen before. Three separate implant-activated padlocks connected a series of stout cables wound around it. Squeezing out through the front door, it bumped against the sill.

"Be careful with that thing!" Dalmeon Geanar ordered. "Can't you see it's fragile? And watch out for my pseudophilodendron! Hurry up, or it'll be late!"

"Take it easy, doc," the gorilla answered. "There's a shuttle leavin' every hour on the—"

Geanar purpled, and only in part, Berdan knew, at mention of the small ships which the old man, as a former Broach technician, trusted less than the instantaneous transport they were built to establish between the planet and *Tom Edison Maru*. Whatever Grandfather was up to, it must be urgent for him to consider using a shuttle.

"Who do you think you're talking to? I'm not paying for your lip! I'm paying you to do as I tell you!"

"You ain't payin' us enough, doc. Cool down or you can do the muscle work yourself."

As they vanished through the membrane, the human partner shook his head and muttered "Sheesh!"

When they'd gone, Geanar strode through the open membrane of his room, expecting Berdan to follow. When he did, what he saw on the bed astounded him further. The old man, who never went anywhere, had his suitcase—for as long as Berdan could remember it had lain on a shelf in the closet between two bags of plant food, gathering dust—half filled with clothing and other personal items.

"I'm going on a business trip." Geanar made it an announcement without looking around at his grandson. At the same time, he folded a brand-new smartsuit, an item of apparel Berdan hadn't even known his grandfather possessed, and laid it atop the other items in the suitcase.

"While I'm gone—no, you won't be going with me—you'll have to take care of yourself. When I get back, things will be different. At long last I'll be somebody. Somebody important! We can move out of this dump and get a decent place to live in a decent sector of the ship—maybe even go back to Earth! I'll hire you a tutor and you can quit watching commercial education channels!"

Five minutes later, without so much as advising the boy about watering the plants, feeding them, or leaving them alone, he, too, had vanished through the front door membrane.

Berdan had been left behind.

Chapter IV:

Happy Birthday, Berdan

The silence was deafening.

It took Berdan a long while to regain his composure. From experience, he knew it would be even longer before he'd assimilated everything that had happened today.

So far today, he corrected.

It seemed to him he'd never been able to experience the right emotion at the right time, only realizing afterward, sometimes as much as several days, he'd been happy, satisfied, or proud of something he'd accomplished. Now, everything on which he'd ever based any sense of normality had been reversed within the space of minutes (a half-conscious reference to his implant told him it was just coming up on noon) and he wondered, and in the same instant regretted having thought to ask, what else could happen to him before this day was over.

He didn't want to know.

Shaking his head, he took the three short steps necessary to take him through the artificial jungle of the apartment into its cooking area—contiguous with the living room and too small to be described with any accuracy as a kitchen—and peered into the refrigerator. Removing a bright-colored plastic package, the contents of which would have upset Mr. Meep, he popped it into the microwave. With a glance back toward the greenery-filled living room area and an appropriate command from his implant, a small section of the carpet began rising, changing color and texture, until a comfortable armchair and coffee table stood where seconds before only empty floor had been visible.

The microwave signalled.

Berdan removed his lunch, a mammothburger with cheese and yamfries, now sizzling hot, summoned up an Osceola Cola from the sink dispenser, went to the armchair, and sat down in a position— more or less on the back of his neck—which would have drawn a sharp remark from his grandfather about posture. He was hungry, but long minutes went by without his eating. The cheeseburger grew cold, the yamfries even greasier than they'd started out, the carbonated soft drink flat, and the ice within it turned to meltwater. Meanwhile, he concentrated his thoughts.

What was going on?

Grandfather, after years of going nowhere and doing nothing—at least this was the impression Berdan had, although by now he wasn't sure of anything—had, without warning, turned into a dynamo. Having refused for what seemed to be forever, not only had the old man permitted his grandson to get a job (Berdan made a mental note—a literal possibility with an implant—to call Mr. Meep to make sure the job was still his), but he seemed to have gotten one himself.

Something which involved sudden business planetside and a massive, coffin-sized shipping crate.

Not altogether conscious of it, Berdan rose to his feet, at the same time struggling with his conscience. He'd like to know more—what was in that crate?—but, being a child of his culture, he was reluctant to invade his grandfather's privacy. Although it was fair to say the old man had never shown much respect for his—Berdan's—privacy, the boy recognized this to be the rationalization it was. He also understood two wrongs don't make a right.

Humanity, however, would never have made any progress if curiosity weren't a stronger force, in particular in fifteen-year-old boys, than culture. His congealing lunch ignored now on the temporary coffee table which wouldn't go away again unless its load were removed, Berdan swallowed his conscience and stepped through the still-dilated door membrane into Dalmeon Geanar's bedroom.

The die, as someone had once observed in somewhat similar circumstances, was cast.

At first Berdan stood motionless in the precise center of the small room, both hands thrust into his smartsuit pockets in a final, futile gesture to his ruptured scruples. The place was just as filled with hanging and potted plants as the area outside, and it was difficult to take it in with a single glance.

The bed had made itself, of course. The closet had retrieved and hung up whatever clothes his grandfather hadn't taken with him and seemed to be busy cleaning them—Berdan could hear a faint ionic hum from that direction. The windows on all four walls and the ceiling were blank, unprogrammed, the place devoid of any clues he might have hoped to find. Curious or not, the boy couldn't bring himself to open any of the dresser drawers—it didn't occur to him this was a strange place to draw the line, having once violated someone else's privacy—but he wondered where the big crate had stood. In the daytime, his grandfather almost never closed his bedroom door, but Berdan hadn't noticed it before this.

Maybe it had just arrived today.

Casting aside everything he regarded as decent behavior, Berdan opened the closet. On first inspection, as the cleaning hum died, no trace remained of the crate, although room enough was left for it. Everything was as it should be, neat, spotless. Overhead, coiled tight against the ceiling, the closet's retrieval tentacle gleamed in the dim light. Whatever their other failings, the housemice, golfball-sized cyberdevices similar to the tentacle, had done a commendable job wiping out their natural prey, the dustbunny, along with every other trace of dirt the carpet peristalsis didn't take care of. An empty space remained at the right, toward the back, where the crate might have stood on its end.

With his head deep in his grandfather's closet, Berdan frowned. What was that in the corner? In the dark recess he couldn't make it out. A mental nudge from his implant caused the walls to emit a soft, illuminating glow. Toward the floor, caught in an upper edge of the base molding—cheap to begin with and starting now to separate from the wall it had been glued to—he saw a scrap of plastic. Berdan squatted down, reached around, and retrieved it.

About the size of a business card, it seemed to be a label—half of a label, anyway; Berdan could see two brittle strips of amber glue along the back—which had somehow been torn from the crate:

Spoonbender's Museum of Scientific Curiosit
   —And Friendly Finance Compa
     A. Hamilton Spoonbe
22-24 Ponsie Stree
      N.

The boy wasn't stupid; his memory, even without the help of an implant, was good; and in most instances he was unafraid to follow wherever the facts led him. Without getting up, he keyed his implant to the first infochannel it locked onto, the electronic equivalent of the newspaper Captain Forsyth had been reading in the park. As usual, he selected a written format, rather than talking-heads-with-pictures. It was easier to get the unvarnished truth that way without the interpretive "assistance" of waggled eyebrows or suggestive tones of voice.

In moments, the words began crawling past his eyes, hanging in the air a few inches before his face.

A spokesbeing for Griswold's Security told Infopeek this morning he was unable to explain why a thief, employing molecular interpenetration programs normally used by the ship's transport system, broke into a seventh level museum last night, apparently for no other reason than stealing a worthless, possibly dangerous memento of a decade-old scientific experiment which culminated in two deaths.

"Some folks just have ghoulish interests, I guess," Captain Burris Griswold asserted, claiming the break-in at Spoonbender's Museum of Scientific Curiosities, 22-24 Ponsie Street, Sector 270, was the first crime of its kind in the eighteen years he has been a security subcontractor aboard *Tom Edison Maru*. Expressing doubt the thief would ever be caught, he said there is "only so much sapient beings can do" and, in his words, "Griswold's is a property-protecting company, not in the business of collecting people, not even crooks."

Contacted at home, museum owner A. Hamilton Spoonbender would not respond to questions. Infopeek has learned that the stolen object was an experimental smartsuit, centerpiece of the museum's collection, originally developed by Laporte Paratronics, Ltd. and considered a failure after two researchers were killed during its testing.

For more Infopeek info on the Spoonbender Museum, Griswold's Security, crime aboard *Tom Edison Maru*, or the experimental smartsuit's tragic history, request Sidebar Series 2335. An additional 50 gr. AG charge will be added to the accounts of nonsubscribers.

A handful of stillpix had been published with the story: a holo of the front of Spoonbender's Museum (to Berdan it looked more like the pawnshop it also claimed to be); a candid three-dimensional portrait of Captain Burris Griswold, a tough-looking character whose expression sent a shiver down the boy's spine; one of A. Hamilton Spoonbender himself, whose flamboyant moustache and eyebrows curled up on the ends; and a picture of the smartsuit itself, still in its tall, transparent display case—about the same size as his grandfather's crate—looking as if it had been fabricated out of mirror-polished titanium or chromium rather than the plain, rubbery gray synthetic to be expected.

Berdan didn't have fifty silver grains to summon up the sidebars which might have told him more. Some services aboard *Tom Edison Maru* came free, as part of a crewbeing's or resident shareholder's benefits. Others had to be paid for. News service, whether it was worth it or not, all but the sketchiest front page headline sort of stuff he'd just accessed, was one of the latter.

Come to think of it, now that his grandfather had departed, he wasn't certain how much money he had. An instant, inward glance at the family "checkbook"—Berdan was in charge of paying bills, also buying groceries and household supplies—told him the worst: Dalmeon Geanar had departed after withdrawing every last silver ounce in their account. The rent on their apartment hadn't been paid yet this month, nor any of the utilities. Berdan was on his own, with what he earned at Mr. Meep's—not payable until next week and not a tenth of what he needed—to tide him over until his grandfather came back.

If he came back.

As he crouched, half in and half out of the old man's closet, both knees beginning to hurt, both legs beginning to fall asleep with the loss of circulation, it was neither physical pain nor anticipated financial distress bothering him. He still wanted, very much, to read more about the experimental smartsuit stolen from Spoonbender's Museum. No doubt lingered in his mind about who the two researchers were who'd been killed testing the device.

But what could be dangerous about a smartsuit?

And why would anyone—without jumping to any undue conclusions, he also felt confident he knew who the thief had been—why would his grandfather want to steal one?

And, Berdan thought about himself, what could he do about it if he were right? Who'd listen to him? He was just a fifteen-year-old kid, after all, without any money, in all probability without any job, and without a leg to stand on where his guesses were concerned. A surmise, he appreciated (and in this he was ahead of many adults), even based on the strongest of feelings, wasn't the same as a fact.

Knees stiff, Berdan began to get to his feet. Maybe the best thing was to tell Mr. Meep about the whole thing. Maybe the old chimpanzee could tell him what to—

"*Ow!*"

Berdan had hit his head again, this time on the underside of an overhanging closet shelf. All sorts of odds and ends which had been stored on it began tumbling down onto his surprised and unprotected shoulders. The worst, amidst a hailstorm of rolled-up socks, sweaters, underwear, and spare shoes, was a sizable box, upholstered in thick, coarse-grained reddish leather, which struck him on the upper arm, leaving what he was sure would be a bruise. If it had fallen on his head, he thought, he'd have been knocked out cold.

Being as neat as he could, Berdan began putting everything back. The box—more of a briefcase than anything else—was fastened shut by means of some sort of powerful, hidden catch. The thing possessed no visible outer locks nor any hinges. He shrugged and was just about to slide it back in place, as well, when he noticed, above the handle, a name embossed in the leather and inlaid in gold:

MacDougall Bear

This had belonged to his father!

Beneath the swiveling luggage handle a metal plate, two inches on a side with a shallow, bowl-shaped depression in its center, had been set into the leather. Having absorbed most of what he knew, like all kids everywhere, from adventure stories his implant summoned up for him, he recognized an old-fashioned thumbprint-activated lock. Which meant, of course, since his father was long dead, no one had ever been able to open this case again without destroying it. And themselves in the process if spy movies contained any truth at all.

Still, Berdan wondered what was in the case. It was heavy enough. Some great weight inside shifted back and forth, but without much noise, when he tilted it. He laid an idle right thumb in the depression, and was astonished when he heard a dull clank and the top of the case popped partway open.

Berdan sat down on the floor again, this time well outside the closet, where the light was better and there were fewer long, hanging leaves to tickle the back of his neck. He laid the leather case in his lap, pivoting the lid back all the way. Inside, on top, was a large yellow plastic envelope with the inscription:

For Berdan Bear on His Twelfth Birthday

Berdan Bear: although he'd been told this was the name he'd been born with, the boy couldn't remember anybody ever calling him by it. It wasn't such a bad name, at that. When his parents had died, his grandfather had adopted him and...*but his twelfth birthday had been three years ago!* With shaking hands—and without noticing what else might be inside the case under the thin cover of tissue plastic which had rested beneath the envelope—Berdan turned back the flap.

* * *

Dear Son,

You can't know, of course, why I pressed your baby thumb into a briefcase lock this morning before leaving for the lab and will never remember I did it. It's probably a silly, unnecessary precaution, but there's some amount of risk in everything worthwhile, and the suit design still has a couple of hoops to jump through.

Anyway, just to make sure, I'll strap on my second-best until the final testing's over with, and leave this with your grandfather. If anything unexpected happens—not likely at this point—he can hold onto it until you're old enough to learn to use it wisely. Your mother and I have made other provisions, financial ones so you'll never have to worry, but this is personal.

We both love you.

Your father,
Mac

The tissue-plastic crinkled, loud in the empty room, covering up other noises Berdan wouldn't have wanted anyone to hear. After a while he wiped his eyes on a sleeve and began unwrapping whatever his father's briefcase contained.

Inside the thin plastic lay, rolled up upon itself, a wide, heavy belt of the same color and texture as the case. Along its length were flap-lidded pockets, at least a dozen of them, containing one unfamiliar artifact after another. Berdan recognized an inertial compass and a big, unpowered folding knife.

The belt hadn't been cut straight, however, and it supported more than just a series of utility pockets. From the right-hand side, where the leather had been formed into a gentle, low-hanging curve, an open-topped holster had been suspended.

And in the holster, dark-finished and deadly-looking, rested the bulk, inert at present, of an enormous fusion-powered Borchert & Graham five megawatt plasma pistol.

Chapter V:

Spoonbender's Museum

The place did look more like a pawnshop than a museum as Berdan paced the sidewalk just outside the door, trying to make up his mind. In one hand he held a small zippered Kevlar bag containing everything he owned and cared about. From the other hung the leather-covered briefcase containing his father's Borchert & Graham.

No closer to a decision, he pushed through the membrane, hearing the annunciator—music, he supposed someone might insist on calling it—burst forth with Wagner's *Valkyrie* played on a row of bicycle horns, in all probability by a trained seal, accompanied by an entire orchestra of bagpipes.

A few feet in front of him stood a partition with two doors, one at either end of the small room the partition formed, and a single, barred, arch-topped ticket window. The wall itself was a riot of color and motion, ablaze with giant holograms.

Spoonbender's Museum of Scientific Curiosities
—And Friendly Finance Company—
Checks Cashed—Loans Arranged
Music Systems Installed—Computers Repaired
Fine Art While-U-Wait
We Also Walk Dogs

* * *

40

The advertisement was repeated many times in several dozen different languages, not all of which were human in origin or which Berdan recognized. From behind the small counter at the window, a wrinkled, ropy, carrot-colored periscope with a black faceted lens the size of Berdan's fist, peered out at the boy. "*Sorry, we're closed today—deliveries at the rear!*"

Berdan dropped his overnight bag and the briefcase and slapped both palms over his ears. It felt as though someone had stabbed his eardrums with a pair of icepicks.

"Oh, I'm *extremely* sorry!"

What had been an excruciating high-pitched squeal now became a normal-sounding human baritone, almost a bass. The orange periscope rose with a series of jiggling motions until Berdan could see it was rooted in what looked like an old-fashioned army helmet, painted fluorescent pink. From beneath its bottom edge a fringe of rubbery gray-green protuberances undulated as the freenie they belonged to, and whom they served as feet and hands, climbed up the ramp built for it behind the counter, crossed the surface to the window bars, and stuck its periscope neck and glittering eye out from between them.

"Please forgive me sir or madam, I was just speaking to my mother on the 'com and forgot to downshift frequencies. I hope I haven't caused you too much discomfort."

Sir or madam indeed. Berdan was indignant. Any member of a species boasting seventeen sexes—he wondered which of its parents the creature counted as its mother—ought to be able to tell the difference between a mere two.

"That's all right," Berdan answered the freenie. "I, uh…I'd like to speak to Mr. Spoonbender."

"Wait there a minute," the freenie suggested. "We really are closed today—burglarized last night and taking inventory for insurance—but I'll see if the boss is busy."

The alien trundled toward the ramp, stopped, and looked back at Berdan, its voice now a whisper. "Actually, he's hardly ever busy. The rest of us do all the work around here."

"Tell him it may be about your burglary."

The freenie nodded its periscope at Berdan and disappeared down the ramp. The boy was left alone with his thoughts and the colorful holographic signs. Something more than a minute later, the door on the right dilated and a tall man in distinctive clothing whom Berdan recognized from the Infopeek stillpix emerged.

"A. Hamilton Spoonbender?" Berdan asked.

Tall, with wavy brown hair, short beard, and a fantastic, curled moustache, the man wore a work shirt, frock coat, real Levis—not just an illusory suit pattern—a battered top hat, and, on the end of his nose, rimless spectacles which Berdan suspected were, unlike Geeky Kehlson's, more than an affectation. Above the lenses, his eyes gleamed in a manner the boy would have described as benignly crazed. In his hand he held a smoking meerschaum carved in his own likeness. The lobby was soon filled with a heavy tobacco aroma.

"*The* Hamilton Spoonbender," he replied, "than whom there is no other. At your service, sir. Walk this way and we'll talk business while I try to sort out a sorry mess."

If the outside of the museum looked like a pawnshop, the inside was like a junkyard, and had doubtless looked this way long before the burglary. Paratronic components spilling out of their cabinets in bewildering tangles stood side by side with painted carousel horses and wonderful, carved musical instruments. A pottery kiln and some kind of metal-melting pot competed for space with a band saw, drill press, table saw, horizontal and vertical mill, and a lathe.

To Berdan, it was like examining the working area of a flint knapper, as if molecular fabrication—spray-painting—had never been invented. A flock of stuffed bats hung from the rafters. In a corner, the remains of a taxidermized Vespuccian sandgator were locked in permanent death-struggle with those of a Sodde Lydfan rotorbird. Scattered about the huge room Berdan could make out at least a hundred semifinished projects, tools and parts lying on bench tops amidst plastic sawdust, metal shavings, and scraps of other materials.

Even above the odor of Spoonbender's meerschaum, Berdan could smell the streaked and grimy coffee machine which stood in the corner with the sandgator and the rotorbird. Here and there, at one bench or another across the vast, disorganized, and cluttered shop, looking less like workers and more like tornado victims searching the rubble for their belongings, Berdan saw half a dozen beings of assorted species. Everywhere he looked, coffee cups stood in various conditions, some full, some empty, some in between. Several were full of peculiar, fuzzy orange mold.

"This delightful creature…" When they'd made their way to the middle of the workshop, Berdan's host removed the pipe from his mouth and took the gauntleted arm of a short, plump, cheerful-looking woman with a welding mask pushed back onto the top of her head. "…is my lady wife, Vulnavia Spoonbender."

"*The* Vulnavia Spoonbender?" Berdan inquired, taking the small hand she offered and shaking it.

"*Touché*—one point for the kid. And, speaking of kids, these young ruffians…" Raising his voice to a shout, Spoonbender pointed to a pair of boys a year or two younger than Berdan, busy carving a fifteen-foot totem pole with chain saws. "…are my sons, Shemp and Curley."

The chain saws stopped.

As one, the boys protested, "Aw, c'mon, Dad!"

"Very well, as you like it: N.O. Spoonbender and N.T. Spoonbender, esquires. May I also present my esteemed associates, Miss Nredmoto *Ommot* Uaitiip, Mr. Rob-Allen Mustache, and Mr. Hum Kenn, whose acquaintance you've already made."

Berdan was somehow certain "N.O." and "N.T." stood for "Number One" and "Number Two" sons, respectively. Ommot was a lamviin, female judging by the stress Spoonbender had placed on her middle name, the first individual of the species Berdan had ever seen in person. She was just putting the finishing touches on a wax sculpture of Sherlock Holmes. Mustache was a chimpanzee; where had he ever gotten a name like that? Hum Kenn was the freenie who'd almost deafened him.

His coffee cup was spotless, filled to the brim, and steaming.

"And you, sir, are—"

Spoonbender's eye fell on the leather case Berdan had put on a counter in order to shake hands all around.

"But I can see, you're *the* MacDougall Bear." A puzzled expression passed over the man's features. He shook his head, accepted the cup of coffee his wife had brought him, and sipped at it in an absent manner, dismissing whatever thought had caused his confusion. He set the cup on a bench.

"Delighted to meet you, sir. How may we be of service?"

Berdan, however, failed to hear the question because, not far away, where it hadn't caught his eye in all the confusion, standing in its tall glass case, just as he'd seen it on the Infopeek program, he spied the chromium glass of the experimental smartsuit he'd thought his grandfather had stolen.

"Put your jaw back in place, Earthling," Ommot told Berdan. "It's only a replica."

"She's right," Rob-Allen Mustache agreed, "one I cast from pewter a few weeks ago."

His synthesizer emitted a sigh. "Wish we had the real thing back."

"Indeed," Spoonbender added, "and I wish it could do everything it was supposed to have—"

"And if we had some ham," Hum Kenn interrupted in a sarcastic, nasal tone, "we could have some ham and eggs—if we had some eggs."

"My dear Kenn," Spoonbender suggested, "why don't you—Great Albert's Ghost! *That's* where I heard the name! *The* MacDougall Bear—and you'd be his son?"

Berdan hadn't had a chance yet to straighten them all out about his name. On the other hand, what did it matter? He was MacDougall Bear's son, after all.

He nodded. "That's right, Mr. Spoonbender. I heard about the burglary and thought I'd come and see…" He wasn't sure what he'd come here to do. He didn't want to accuse his grandfather outright, not to a third party.

One small idea in the back of his mind had pushed him through the door: selling his father's pistol, so he could pursue the old man and discover the truth. But he'd never done anything like this before. He wasn't sure whether he wanted to or not. The pistol was the one thing his father had managed to leave him.

He spoke. "I was raised by my grandfather, Mr. Spoonbender, and never knew much about my father and mother. I came to find out more, especially about how they died."

Mrs. Spoonbender frowned, as if she were thinking about her own sons growing up without mother or father. With an abrupt movement, she flipped the dark-visored helmet into place and went back to her welding. Berdan heard her sniff back a tear behind the mask.

In the embarrassed silence that followed, Ommot offered Berdan a cup of coffee—it seemed to be the tribal custom in this place—which, being as polite as he could about it, he refused.

"The Brightsuits..." Spoonbender mused, appearing to be speaking more to himself than to anybody in the room. "It's said three of them were created to begin with, prototypes, years in the making. Two of them were destroyed, and the last, which I bought as surplus, had been built as an emergency backup. They all possessed certain features which, at least in theory, would have allowed instantaneous transport through space—"

"—without," Ommot interrupted, "benefit of a spaceship—"

Spoonbender ignored the lamviin.

"—using its own inertialess tachyon drive system."

"An extremely *compact* inertialess tachyon drive system," Hum Kenn offered.

"Which, of course," Rob-Allen Mustache tossed in, "could also be used as a weapon—"

"Rendering the suit's wearer virtually omnipotent!" Spoonbender concluded.

"Except," Vulnavia Spoonbender—her nose red and her cheeks streaked with tears—flipped her welding visor back, "when it killed the wearer, instead."

"Quite so." A. Hamilton Spoonbender sighed. "I suppose, under the circumstances, the boy's entitled to hear the entire story. Where's my coffee cup?"

"Right on the bench in front of you!" said everybody except Berdan at the same time.

Even now, the details weren't clear.

Covered with near-microscopic propulsive tachyon laser cells and generating a field which cancelled its inertia, the Brightsuit, as Spooner had called it, ought to have succeeded, accelerating its wearer to velocities exceeding that of light. The principle was well-established and simple—it was what drove the *Tom Edison Maru* through the galaxy—although more miniaturized than ever before. It was unfortunate that well-established, simple principles sometimes produce differing results in differing circumstances.

During a routine final test, two of the suits, MacDougall's and Erissa's, had been destroyed in a cataclysmic explosion, leaving not one atom clinging to another. Unable, after two years of investigation, to determine what had caused the tragedy, Laporte Paratronics had abandoned further experiments, salvaged the third suit's 'com gear (the only portion not integral with the new design—Spoonbender claimed they'd been afraid to try further dismantling), and sold the suit for scrap prices, demanding a waiver of liability from the purchaser.

Spoonbender had bought it for exhibit in the museum he maintained—and which Berdan hadn't yet seen—next door to his workshop. The boy also suspected the man harbored dreams of trying to solve the technical riddle it presented—or had, before the inexplicable theft of the otherwise worthless artifact.

"Somehow," Berdan told Spoonbender when the story—what there had been of it—was finished, I'm going to recover that suit, for personal reasons. That's why I'm here."

Berdan felt bad, not telling his new friends about his grandfather but thought it just as well. He was beginning to believe the old man must have been desperate to make some kind of mark in a universe where he felt he was regarded with contempt, and, whatever else he might think about it, it was private family business. Let them think his reasons had only to do with his mother and father.

"The trouble is, Mr. Spoonbender, I've never done anything like this before. To tell the truth…" He thought, with that same old sinking feeling, about the failed desserts at Mr. Meep's. "I've never managed to do much of anything at all, and I don't know how to start."

"Upon the incomparably beautiful planet of Sodde Lydfe where I was born and reared," Ommot suggested, a ripple passing through her fur, "a backwater podunk of the quintessential order and a terrific place to be *from*, we've a saying: '*Grot yt siidaikmo ad yt hai's, dit yt nydviimon, niivdoef eth nrais.*'"

"Which means?"

A suspicious expression dragged Spoonbender's bushy eyebrows into near-collision.

"Roughly translated," Mustache replied, "'If at first you don't succeed, cut your throat and watch it bleed.'"

"But Berdan hasn't even begun yet!" one of the Spoonbender scions protested.

"Maybe," said the other one, "Ommot means 'Give up now and avoid the last-minute rush.'"

Ommot's fur drooped. "It was merely an attempt at raffish, Earthian humor, intended to raise his spirits and stiffen his moral fiber. Something must have been lost in the translation."

"Well, by Lysander Spooner's long and snowy beard," Spoonbender swore to Berdan, "I'd certainly pay you a modest quittance to get the Brightsuit back. How might that affect your spirits and your moral fiber? Nothing lavish, I'd give you to understand, but something equitable. And generally one initiates such an undertaking—only a figure of speech, of course—by assessing one's capital assets. Briefly, and in the vernacular, you got any bread, son?"

With reluctant fingers, Berdan opened his father's briefcase and handed Spoonbender the plasma gun.

"I have this."

"Well I'll be a monk—" Spoonbender stopped, glanced up at Rob-Allen Mustache, and cleared his throat. "Er, a dirty bird. A genuine Model 247 B&G! A veritable captain's sidearm! I'd have this removed, though."

He pointed at the butt of the pistol to a lanyard swivel, clinking and rattling as he turned the weapon over in his hands.

"Much too noisy when stealth might be better advised."

"I need..." Berdan hesitated, embarrassed. "I mean, I thought maybe you might want to buy it from me for your museum or at least lend me money against it."

Spoonbender laid the fusion-powered pistol back in the briefcase and examined the boy over the tops of his spectacles, said nothing, but instead picked up the heavy gun belt and subjected it to scrutiny, letting the leather run through his hands. At one point he stopped, with a brief grunt of surprise.

At long last, he spoke. "Son, I know I'm going to hate myself for this in the morning, but what you really need is a recharge and some gun-handling and shooting lessons. You've no need at all to sell this fabulous weapon or to borrow money from anyone."

Berdan moved closer. "How's that?"

"Observe..." Spoonbender ran a thumbnail along the top of the belt, where it parted and the lining peeled back of its own accord. Between the layers, a long row of large coins had been concealed, each over a quarter of an inch thick, at least an inch and a half in diameter, bearing the portrait of the heavy-bearded historic president every Confederate recognized, and made of solid gold.

"...twenty-four, twenty-five, twenty-six, twenty-seven! Two-ounce gold superlysanders, minted by Gary's Bait & Trust late in the last century. Relatively rare and hardly the most convenient of denominations, but, my boy, you're a wealthy man!"

Berdan's mind reeled. Just thirty seconds before, he'd been destitute and desperate. Now, he realized two things. First, he owed a great deal to the honesty of this peculiar individual, who might have bought his father's pistol for a song and never told him about the gold. Second, MacDougall Bear hadn't been altogether trusting of Dalmeon Geanar and had supplemented the financial arrangements he and Erissa had made through the old man for their son's future.

Reaching out, Berdan plucked three coins—as close to ten percent as he could get—from the pliable lining which, over the years, had molded itself to the metal disks.

"Mr. Spoonbender, you've given me valuable information, and I believe I owe you—"

Spoonbender assumed a melodramatic posture and let his eyes flash with theatrical anger. "Sirrah, you impugn my motives, insult my integrity, dishonor my ancestors, and..."

"Sully your escutcheon?" Rob-Allen Mustache suggested.

Spoonbender glared at the chimpanzee. "I was getting to that."

His expression softened as he turned back to Berdan. "Besides, kid, you need the money, and your daddy intended you to have it. Many heartfelt thanks for the kind thought, but virtue is its own punishment."

Berdan blinked. "Don't you mean, 'virtue is its own reward'?"

Spoonbender gazed down at the gleaming coins and sighed. "Believe me, son, I know exactly what I'm saying."

Chapter VI:

Hot Pursuit

Not quite two hours had passed since Dalmeon Geanar had departed the small apartment he shared with his grandson in the wake of a large, mysterious crate.

To Berdan, left on his own for the first time in his life, it seemed like an eternity.

He'd spent some uncounted amount of time trying to decide whether his suspicions about his grandfather—that the old man had stolen the fabulous Brightsuit—were justified, more time figuring out what to do about it, and almost an hour in the congenial bedlam of Spoonbender's Museum and Friendly Finance Company.

Now, having succeeded where Diogenes had failed, and having obtained some useful advice from the honest man he'd found, Berdan was on his own again. Making his way toward the Broach depot on the lowest level of the ship, he wished he felt up to wearing the broad, heavy gun belt which, instead, he still carried in the briefcase where his father had left it for him over a decade ago. The trouble was—and it seemed to Berdan this typified everything he was going through at the moment—he knew nothing about operating the Borchert & Graham plasma pistol it had been built for (he couldn't even tell if the thing was loaded, let alone shoot it), and didn't have any time to learn.

In the same sense, trying as he was to catch up with his grandfather, trying to discover the truth about the old man's activities and about the experimental smartsuit he appeared to have stolen, Berdan didn't have the faintest idea how to accomplish those things either and, again, didn't have time to learn.

Nevertheless, if he didn't do something, it would soon be too late—if it wasn't already. For once in his otherwise cautious life, it appeared to him the proper course consisted of leaping before he looked. He might fall on his face or into a hole, but nothing was going to get accomplished any other way.

Berdan's hesitant footsteps—and a complicated series of trips through the *Tom Edison Maru*'s transport system—brought him at last to the lowest level in the ship. As usual—although Berdan had no way of recognizing it—he was preoccupied and therefore unconscious of the wonderful sights surrounding him.

The size of a small city, over seven and a half miles from rim to rim, the full diameter of the starship, this level accommodated far more than just a few hundred Thorens Broach terminals, those wondrous devices capable of transmitting passengers and cargo across space-time in an instant. Overhead, a huge transparent bubble permitted an amazing view—from the sandy bottom of *Tom Edison Maru*'s second level indoor ocean. Drawn to the warm light coming from below—or perhaps to the many fish attracted by the light (or the opulent plant growth it engendered)—a giant squid rolled over and across the curved outer surface of the bubble, reaching out an occasional long and lazy tentacle to snag a swimming snack and stuff it into his parrot-beaked mouth.

Berdan walked by beneath this incredible spectacle and never even knew it existed.

Here in *Tom Edison Maru*'s basement, many other things were going on as well. This was where the ship's auxiliary craft—shuttles such as Geanar had been hurrying to get aboard—were based. Miniatures of the giant dome-shaped interstellar craft herself, they nestled into her flattened underside, blending into her outline and contributing the output of their tachyon lasers to her own.

All along Berdan's path airlocks holo-decorated with advertising urged him to hire the services of this or that shuttlecraft. He walked right by without noticing a thing.

Away from the mother ship, the shuttles left behind great inverted bowl-shaped empty docking bays in her underside. The largest of these auxiliary craft, seven of them in all, carried seven smaller craft in the same manner. Each of these tertiary vessels housed seven even smaller vessels, and so on, from the giant starship down to scouting machines which carried a single passenger.

It never occurred to Berdan, who'd grown up in the Confederacy, to wonder why a civilization with something like the Thorens Broach needed starships and auxiliaries. While a Broach could reach out from its anchor point in time and space to place people and cargo anywhere within a range of several light years, it was difficult, dangerous, and expensive to do so without a second, receiving station at the destination end. Most of the smaller spaceships were equipped, as their primary function, to carry and install such a receiving station.

Others did preliminary exploration.

The driving machinery—no more than a turn of phrase, since it contained not a single moving part—of the *Tom Edison Maru* herself was to be found on this lowest level, along with everything required to maintain her environment and accomplish her mission: circulation pumps, filtration plants, chemical refineries, and fusion reactors. In this sense, the ship was rather like any of the vast industrial cities of Earth or her better developed colonies.

This was the one portion of *Tom Edison Maru* where one was always aware—unless one was a fifteen-year-old boy on a desperate mission of his own—he was aboard a starship, itself a giant machine, pulsing and throbbing with more pent-up energy than humanity had expended during the first ten thousand years of its Earthbound history.

Berdan, however, and even his less-preoccupied fellow travelers, were given small opportunity to see any of this. Stepping out of the final transport patch his implant had directed him to, he faced what, to an inhabitant of an earlier age, would have seemed like a huge hotel lobby or airport terminal, surrounded at its perimeter by an endless bank of small, glass-sided booths.

Here and there, people were entering these booths and disappearing. At the opposite end of the terminal, heavy-wheeled containerized loads were being guided into double- and quadruple-sized booths. Elsewhere, a smaller number of individuals were appearing inside certain booths, to all appearances from nowhere, and coming out into the terminal area, most of them with a look of relief on their faces.

Berdan noticed this much and shuddered, wondering what it must be like down there on the planet Majesty, which *Tom Edison Maru* was orbiting.

Along the center of the enormous room, a series of several circular information desks was manned—or, rather, *beinged*—by living entities of several species, ready to answer questions and solve problems for the Broach company's customers. It was an old-fashioned touch, but, like Mr. Meep's insistence on live waiters, one which lent a friendly, personal feeling. It may also have been necessary to encourage nervous first-time Broach passengers.

Berdan, considering himself one of these, was glad to have someone to consult about it. None of them seemed busy at the moment, and he had his choice.

He walked up to the nearest desk.

"May I help you?" The receptionist was a pretty human girl not much older than Berdan himself.

"I hope so. I want to go planetside, or whatever you say, to Majesty. How do I do it?"

"Do you have any particular destination in mind? And please don't just repeat 'planetside' or 'Majesty'—that's a whole world down there, you know."

"Well," he told her, "it's like this: my grandfather took one of the shuttles, but…" Berdan hesitated, uncomfortable and aware he was treading on someone's rights to personal privacy.

Again.

The girl, accustomed to some hesitation on the part of certain of her clientele, was patient with Berdan, although she might not have been if she'd known the reason. "Yes?"

"Er, I thought I'd surprise him, that is if I could find out where he went."

The girl looked at Berdan in an odd way, but without, he hoped, too much suspicion. "Your grandfather, you say."

"Yes, ma'am. Dalmeon Geanar, Lindsay Arms Apartments, Number Two-C, Five Eighty-seven Claypool Street, Sector Twenty-nine, Fourth Level. My name's Berdan Geanar.

52

"I'm his grandson."

He realized, just as the last three words came out of his mouth, how stupid and redundant they must have sounded. The girl smiled an apology, although it wasn't her fault, Berdan thought, he couldn't think of anything intelligent to say to her. Girls always had that effect on him, even in the best of circumstances. He'd long ago decided he incurred less risk keeping his mouth shut, although this policy wasn't going to be of much help here and now.

"Well, if you want to surprise him, I guess there isn't much point in calling ahead, is there?"

"No," Berdan agreed. "Can I find out who went down in what shuttles earlier—about two hours ago?"

The girl shook her head. "To tell the absolute truth, the shuttle traffic wasn't very heavy this morning. This is just a stopover, if you know what I mean, a milk run, not a popular or important destination. Just see how few Broaches are being used this afternoon."

In fact, Berdan had noticed he had the whole huge place almost to himself.

"However," the girl continued, "I'm sorry I must inform you none of the shuttle service companies operating aboard *Tom Edison Maru* keep passenger lists. It's a matter of personal privacy, you see. Nobody'd do business with them if they did."

A disappointed expression must have appeared on Berdan's face despite himself, for she hurried on.

"There are only two arrival points on Majesty of any significance, anyway: Geislinger, the settlement at the north pole, and Talisman at the south pole."

Visions of winter hurricanes and glaciers two miles deep swept through Berdan's mind.

"I see. Well…"

"It isn't quite as bad as that."

It was as if the girl could read Berdan's thoughts. She reached down, lifted a heavy, streamlined pistol-shape which had been lying on the counter in front of her, and pointed it at him. Too polite—and far too tongue-tied—to refuse, he let her place the cold, dime-sized muzzle against his forehead.

A *flash!* filled his mind. He relaxed, letting his implant absorb the data, words and pictures the brochure projector contained, and which he'd "read" later when he had the chance.

"Just wait until you get down there," the girl told him. "You'll see. The whole planet's covered by some kind of jungle. The only cleared areas are the poles, and it says here they're almost temperate by human standards. The larger of the two Confederate settlements is Talisman, and it's likeliest your grandfather—"

Berdan's eyes lit with sudden inspiration. "If you don't mind my asking, which of the two is more unsavory—you know, pirates, portside dives, suspicious characters, disreputable bars, and so forth."

Once again, Berdan was depending on all the adventure stories he'd ever seen—and in all probability, he realized, embarrassing himself. The girl peered at Berdan, an odd look of speculation dancing in her eyes (which, he noticed, were a deep, beautiful blue), but she didn't say anything about what she was thinking.

"Hmm. I believe I know what you mean. Local color. Are you absolutely sure—"

"Yeah, I'm sure. I wish I weren't."

"All right, let me see." For a moment her beautiful blue eyes acquired the absent, searching expression typical, on occasions, to implant users. She was looking something up or consulting with somebody. Berdan, a lifelong implant user himself, noticed but saw nothing odd about it, since he often looked the same way himself.

Her eyes focused.

"Okay, Talisman, at the south pole, is definitely the place you want to start with—not the town itself, mind you, which, it says here, is a perfectly respectable place—but a sort of suburb down there they call Watner."

Again the pause and the absent look. "Get yourself a gun, since you're not wearing one, leave most of your money aboard ship in a nice safe bank account, and keep your spare hand on your wallet, anyway."

"Thanks," Berdan replied. "I already have too much gun, which I don't know how to use, will probably need all my money down on Majesty, and, as for spare hands..." He held his up, both of which were full of luggage.

54

The girl smiled and shook her head. "Well in that case, take any of those Broach booths over there, deposit three silver ounces, and tell the implant receptor where you want to go. In theory, you'll come out in another booth, exactly like that one, at the other end."

"Thanks," Berdan replied. "Especially for the 'in theory.' I really needed that. Uh, do you happen to have change for a gold two-ounce superlysander?"

"Nothing's ever easy with you, is it?" She accepted the massive coin from Berdan, one of the three he'd offered Spoonbender, handed him his change—a great deal of it—and a plastic company token.

"Something they won't tell you in the tourist brochures because it's bad for business: watch out for rats. They don't have any natural enemies down there, and the population's exploded, like rabbits in Australia. Now take that to the nearest unoccupied booth, insert it in the lighted slot, and off you go."

And good riddance, Berdan was certain she was thinking. He always seemed to affect girls that way.

He mumbled thanks and followed her instructions. Finding an unoccupied booth was easy, he walked over to the nearest one, set his bag down, slid the transparent folding door back, picked up his bag again and entered the confined space. Setting the bag down once more, he slid the door closed behind him.

On the left wall, a small slot lit up, and he "heard" a voice via his implant. *"Please insert token and specify destination."*

Talisman, he thought, making sure he had both bags in hand again. *I'll try to take the rest by easy stages. Guard your wallet. Learn to shoot. Watch out for rats.*

A small display confirmed his destination had been entered. He inserted the token.

Before him, a blinding, brilliant blue dot appeared on the opposite wall. It expanded into a blue-edged circle which grew until it met the metal edges of the booth. The receiver must have been outdoors: through the aperture he could see the dirt roads, boardwalks, and makeshift buildings of a typical new-colony town.

Ready or not, Dalmeon Geanar, here I come!

He took a breath and stepped forward.

Before his right foot entered the Broach—and before he could stop himself—something crackled.

The picture blurred and shifted.

Berdan pitched forward into a sea of small green leaves and sank in over his head.

As he'd feared, he'd fallen on his face—

And into a hole.

Chapter VII:

THE SEA OF LEAVES

I t was like being dropped into a room full of bright green ping-pong balls.

Berdan didn't sink far into the leafy morass, but without any place to plant his feet, nowhere he could push with his hands, he found he couldn't stand up again. Instead, all he could do was lie on his back, helpless and floundering.

Overhead, the sky of Majesty was a bright and cloudless blue. Everything else, as far as he could see (which, lying in this position, wasn't far) was an endless ocean of green, every possible shade and hue and saturation. Scattered here and there among the leaves were clusters of small, rather disappointed-looking pale green flowers and clumps of berries of about the same size and color.

The air was hot and damp.

All about him wafted the smells of lush vegetation, the sharp tang of the leaves and stems he'd broken, the sweeter breath of new growth, the richer, loamy odor—swampy, like that of just-picked mushrooms—of whatever lay beneath. He dreaded sinking into that organic-smelling darkness, never to resurface.

According to everything he'd seen and heard, the mossy biosphere of Majesty would tolerate no other plant life, but existed in ready symbiosis with countless animal organisms living on or beneath its surface—as if it were the vast, green, living ocean it resembled.

Numerous Earth-native species had been transplanted to Majesty, although often with a kind of success that hadn't always been deliberate. Since the planet's discovery, many types of Earthian animals had found a home in the worldwide moss, including thousands of species of birds, and, it seemed everybody kept telling him, hordes of large ferocious rats.

Watch out for the rats.

By some happy chance, he still held onto both his Kevlar zipper bag and his father's briefcase. With his arms spread wide, they helped to support his weight.

Since he couldn't do much of anything else at the moment, he began deliberate breathing, as slow and deep as he could manage it, feeling his heart beat, willing it to slow, a difficult task in the panic-generating atmosphere of a steambath.

As he relaxed, his brain began to work again. Some of the shock and surprise wore off. Berdan began to be aware of other things besides the sky, the light, and the odors, among them the soft sighing of a gentle breeze rustling what must have been quintillions of miniature leaves paving the entire planet. Maybe, he found himself thinking, with this much vegetation—and not much of anything else—you might even be able to hear the stuff growing. Maybe this was what he heard, or imagined he heard, now: a sort of odd creaking which—

Berdan jumped, as much as he was able to, and almost lost hold of his bags. Breathing, despite himself, in rapid, shallow gasps again, he thought he could feel some small, hard-jointed, many-legged crawly thing on the back of his neck. With careful, slow movements, he drew his outspread arms together, held both handles, bag and briefcase, with one hand—their weight on his chest pushed him down further into the leaves—and reached up with the hand he'd managed to free....

Nothing.

Well, whatever it had been, he'd given it all the time in the world to get away—

—or to squiggle down the back of his suit!

At this spine-chilling thought, Berdan squirmed, sinking deeper with every movement, until the leaves began closing over his face like living quicksand.

Panic threatened to seize him.

He refused to let it.

Again he forced himself to relax, taking deep breaths (after all, he thought, they might be his last, and he might as well enjoy them), and spread his arms out again.

It didn't work.

This stuff wasn't water, or even quicksand for that matter. Even when he settled down, stopped sinking, he didn't float back to the top. It was hopeless. He wouldn't be able to hold still and would go on sinking, deeper every minute, until—

"*Screeeeegh!*"

"*Yaaaaaaagh!*"

Behind him, something much larger than whatever creepy-crawly he'd worried about earlier bellowed and reared up over his head. Berdan screamed at the same time. A shadow fell over his face. Huge and black, it blotted out the sun.

The first, most hideous and lasting impression the thing made on Berdan's mind was of *legs*, thousands upon thousands of legs. The horror rearing above him seemed to be composed of nothing but restless, wiggling, spike-jointed legs.

It was at least as wide as Berdan was tall, about the same color as the vegetation, and smelled like a stack of dinner dishes which had been left in the sink for a week. What he could see of it was twice his height. More, perhaps: he realized, in some remote part of his mind, it must be a great deal longer than it appeared to support the portion standing up among the leaves. Either that or it was built like a bird, a great deal lighter than it looked.

He noticed the jaws, similar in construction to the legs, restless in the same way, three huge, sweeping hooks of shiny, chitinous material, with odd bristly patches and dull-toothed saw edges moist and glistening on their inside surfaces.

The monster opened and shut them as it bent closer to Berdan.

Watch out for the rats?

Let the rats watch out for themselves!

For his own part, the frightened boy was hurrying to get his father's briefcase open, to get at the plasma gun, without losing anything else inside it or his other bag. With panic sweeping through him again, he couldn't remember whether any charge had been left in the pistol. He didn't think so. The handle of his zipper bag was looped over his wrist, interfering as he clawed at the lock of the case—until he remembered he must use his thumb to open it.

The clashing jaws descended.

The nightmarish thing froze. It seemed to glance up, past its intended victim, out across the Sea of Leaves toward some distant threat. It swayed back and forth as if trying to hear or see better—Berdan hadn't noticed whether it had eyes or not—whirled about, and left the helpless boy by himself.

Silence fell once more.

Berdan tried his best to sit up among the leaves to see what sort of unimaginable, horrible thing it had taken to frighten the first monster away. Whatever it was, he didn't want anything to do with it! All he accomplished with the effort, however, was to sink deeper into the vegetation surrounding him. Forcing himself to stillness, he began to hear what the monster had heard first, an eerie whistling noise—several eerie whistling noises—far away but coming closer.

Watch out for the rats.

Groaning with terror and fatigue, he went on groping, trying to get at his father's plasma gun, every wasted, useless motion pushing him deeper into the leaves. Something whiplike, and not green at all, slapped across his fingers.

It felt just like the seminaked tail of a large, energetic rat.

"Hey!" He still hadn't managed to open the briefcase. To Berdan, it felt like a nightmare he suffered all the time where he tried to run faster and faster, only to stay in the same place. Before he could unlock it, the case was snatched out of his hand by what appeared to be a small, eyeless blue-gray velvet-covered snake.

"Hey, cut that out!"

His other bag was wrenched away.

Something—some rough pair of somethings—seized him by both smartsuited ankles.

He'd just become aware of this development, when another pair of blue snakes, identical to the one which had taken his case, wrapped themselves around his wrists, pulling against one another until he was stretched flat on his back again.

He began to rise out of the leaves.

In this position, staring, whether he wanted to or not, at the sky overhead, it was difficult to see what sort of thing or things had grabbed him and his possessions. He was grateful that a snakelike object like the ones around his wrists and ankles hadn't also wrapped itself around his neck. The multiple whistling noises were so loud by now they hurt his ears. They seemed to arise from all around him. With a growl of anger and frustration, he twisted his neck—the attempt was painful—and was rewarded with a peculiar sight.

Each of his outstretched limbs was being held, four or five feet above the ocean of leaves, by a creature which seemed strange, even to a boy used to associating with aliens (and other nonhumans) every day. While it was their limbs—soft-textured, tapering tentacles which had reminded him of velvet-covered snakes—he was in contact with, the principal thing he noticed about each of them was the eye.

Each had only one, but, somehow, it was enough.

It was as if a three-legged starfish had been formed from plasticine modeling clay, the legs stretched as far as the clay could go without tearing, perhaps six or seven feet in total length from tentacle tip to tentacle tip. The imaginary sculptor had sprinkled them with blue-gray flocking and pushed a basketball-sized transparent marble through the center, so it stuck out on both sides.

Berdan could look straight through the creatures.

The one thing obstructing this view as a softball-sized black globular organ hanging in the center of the larger, transparent one. He guessed it served as a retina, the place where light was focused and converted into images.

Berdan remembered he didn't have to guess. He'd absorbed a brochure about this planet just before stepping into the Broach booth. He concentrated, and...

The information burst into his mind in words and bright-colored images: the things carrying him were taflak, the intelligent but primitive natives of this world which Confederates called Majesty. They lived on what they called "the Sea of Leaves," a name for the entire planet in their own curious, whistling tongue. The object at the center of the taflak eye was more than just a retina (although its light-absorbing outer surface served that purpose, too), it was their brain.

And they were supposed to be friendly.

"Hey, you guys!" Berdan wriggled a wrist, trying to attract the attention of one of the taflak carrying him. "Hey, put me down a second, will you?"

The creature ignored him.

He tried the taflak on the other side with the same result.

Two more of the odd natives were helping to carry him. Kicking his legs, however, only caused their fuzzy tentacles to tighten about his ankles until both of his feet began to grow cool and numb and fall asleep. He wondered where they intended taking him, how long this peculiar journey would last, and what they'd do with him when they got there—and was sorry he'd thought to ask.

He also wondered how it was that the taflak, with just three skinny tentacles apiece, somehow managed to keep their heads (a figurative turn of phrase at best) above the weeds, when he himself, with four much broader limbs, had settled toward the center of the planet. The half dozen natives escorting his bearers were even doing cartwheels—revolving limb over limb, while at the same time passing the stubby, long-bladed spears they carried from the tentacle about to hit the "ground" before them to another high above their plump, triangular torsos.

As soon as he'd asked himself this question, he knew from the information his implant had absorbed back aboard ship that the taflak were of much lighter construction than human beings—it was the same idea he'd had about the many-legged monster. For millions of years they'd evolved in this environment, among this infinity of leaves, and the ends of their tentacles splayed into hundreds of fine-stranded supporting "fingers," each over a foot long.

An unassisted human or a simian, without such support, would sink into the denser growth to a depth in the biosphere sufficient to immobilize him, where he'd die of suffocation or starvation (dehydration being inconceivable) if he wasn't eaten alive first by the voracious wildlife rumored to infest it. Berdan's smartsuit might have let him survive—at least until things got around to the "eaten alive" part—but it was old, worn, and had never been subjected to a test like this. He'd never even been able to get the hood, which lay limp and useless across his chest, to fasten around his head in the proper manner.

He could sure use that Brightsuit now, he thought, if he had some ham and eggs.

More than a hundred foolhardy individuals, his implant told him—Confederate, not native taflak—disappeared without a trace on this planet every year.

Watch out for the rats.

His implant also informed him the monstrous beast which had tried to eat him earlier was a "can-can," so called because its long rows of many legs (three in number, two where one would have expected them to be, and a third where most Earth animals kept their backbones) resembled those of a human chorus line. Berdan's life had been in real danger. However, compared to other, more hungry and dangerous things lurking deeper in the Sea of Leaves, the can-can was regarded by the colonists who'd written the brochure as a minor pest, a spoiler of picnics, a tipper-over of garbage cans, in short, a giant thousand-legged cockroach.

Time passed.

The taflak carrying Berdan, while ignoring his attempts to communicate with them (his internal travelogue maintained that many of the Majestan natives spoke intelligible, if somewhat high-pitched, English) loosened their uncomfortable grip on his ankles. One by one their cartwheeling escorts began switching off with them, sharing the burden. As soon as the pins-and-needles tingling went away, he grew so relaxed in this position he surprised himself by dozing off.

As a result, he didn't know how much time had passed—he'd been far too busy to ask his implant what time it was when he'd first fallen into the leaves—when the taflak slowed, took up a new, more excited whistling, and were greeted by several dozen more of their own kind, making the same sorts of sounds.

They'd come to a village.

Dozens of noisy individuals ran out to greet them, some of the greeters perfect miniatures of the hunters who carried Berdan. These small ones wheeled up to examine their find, or chirped at their fathers and elder brothers until they were given the spears to carry the last few steps—or revolutions, Berdan corrected.

Everybody, it seemed, loves a parade.

Having achieved a degree of civilization, the taflak were no longer quite as much at home on the Sea of Leaves—any more than the average human would be in the kind of equatorial jungle where the race evolved—as the can-can. Also, since they employed fire and were obvious toolmakers and users, they required a firmer, more stable base for their activities than the vegetation itself provided.

Thanks to this reasoning and the information he'd absorbed, Berdan wasn't surprised to be carried up a long, sloping ramp onto a large raftlike structure, woven from the dried stems and branches of the single species of plant life on the planet. No doubt its invention had been a major milestone in taflak history.

Atop the woven platform—to Berdan the pattern of its weave resembled some of the checked or shredded cereals he was accustomed to eating for breakfast—from squat beehive-shaped domes of the same material, emerged dozens more of the odd sapients, the taflak equivalent of women, old men, and children, eager, he thought, to see what the hunting party had brought home this time.

Berdan wasn't certain he liked being a trophy.

He was a great deal less happy when, instead of setting him on his feet, now that the security and solidity of the village platform lay beneath them, they paraded him about, pausing at each and every hut so the inhabitants could examine him on their own doorsteps with a giant glassy eye and curious tentacle before his bearers passed on to the next dwelling and the next exhibition. This happened several times before Berdan's patience was exhausted.

"Okay, okay! Enough's enough!"

This time, he struggled much harder than before, flailing both his arms, jerking at the imprisoning tentacles, kicking his legs. The brochure inside his head had been correct in one respect: the taflak were light of build. Although close to his size, he guessed the largest of them weighed no more than thirty or forty pounds, about the weight of a medium-sized dog. Under different circumstances he'd have been waving them around like laundry on a wash line.

The implant, however, had understated their strength—more dismaying than surprising to the boy at present—and the fact that, rooted in the tight-woven matting underfoot, the hundreds of slim tendrils sprouting from the ends of their velvety tentacles made them all but immovable when they wanted to be.

And it appeared, right now, they wanted to be.

"Let me down, you jerks!"

The four taflak, who'd carried him to yet another section of the town raft or platform, obliged him this time. The whistling and chirping of their audience rose to an intolerable level. Stopping, they let him go, dropping the squirming boy into a huge fire-hardened clay cauldron of cold water, around the soot-stained base of which small twigs, dried leaves, and many larger branches had been piled.

While several of the creatures held him in the pot, others formed a spear-bristling ring around it—their spear points directed in, not out—and began to light a fire under it.

A medium-sized taflak rolled up to his side, passing a broad platter from tentacle to tentacle, which it dumped into the pot. Berdan shivered as he stared down at the chopped up berries and shoots bobbing in the water all around him.

Somehow, he had a feeling he wasn't about to take a bath.

Chapter VIII:

PEMOT

lames crackled.

The whistling of the natives grew shriller.

Smoke began rising about the giant cauldron, stinging Berdan's eyes and making him sneeze and cough, as the taflak holding him in the pot backed away from the fire.

Maybe they burned easier than humans, thought the boy, his implant offering him no information on the subject. For whatever reason, it appeared they thought their efforts to restrain him were no longer necessary, that he wouldn't pass over or through the barrier of flame which now surrounded him like a wall. Maybe they'd just never had a dinner impolite enough to get up and walk away.

Well, if that's what they think, they're wrong!

The circle of spear bearers standing around him showed no inclination to move, one way or another. The choice between frying pan and fire, Berdan thought, was easier to make than he'd ever imagined, and the forks—those pointed spears—weren't even worth worrying about. Keeping an eye on them nonetheless, and wincing a bit as the fine hair on the backs of his hands began to singe and crisp away, he seized the edge of the pot, put one foot over, and—

"I say…" These words were followed by a series of whistles, as if the speaker were addressing someone by name.

"Wouldn't you agree we've all had quite enough amusement at this poor young fellow's expense?"

66

Berdan was angrier than he could ever remember being. Ignoring the voice, even though it spoke perfect English, he hopped over the fire, out of the pot, and began kicking at the burning leaves and branches, stamping on the coals to put the fire out.

Something touched his shoulder.

He whirled, teeth gritted, both fists clenched. "Just try it, you—"

"Epots Dinnomm *Pemot*," replied the same voice as before, "late of the sovereign planet Sodde Lydfe, by way of your own green and splendid Earth: taflakologist, itinerant philosopher, observer of the sapient condition, at your service—although, I daresay you thought it more likely to be at your funeral."

By now, Berdan didn't know what he thought. The individual he found standing before him wasn't one of the primitive—and, it appeared, cannibalistic—taflak, but a nine-limbed lamviin, complete with brand-new smartsuit, canvas shoulder bag, a small pistol strapped to one of its upper legs, and, incredible as it was, a monocle four inches in diameter screwed into one eye.

All it lacked to complete the outfit of a gentleman jungle adventurer was a pith helmet.

Berdan had never imagined a being as alien in appearance as one of the lamviin could seem so familiar and welcome to him. Although they were relative newcomers to the Confederacy and a popular subject in the media, he'd met only one other of the species in person, the female sculptor at A. Hamilton Spoonbender's Museum and Friendly Finance Company. Like her, this one—which might have rescued him, if he hadn't rescued himself—stood about three and a half feet tall with a carapace shaped in outline like that of a crab.

An extremely large crab.

Like crabs, Berdan knew, lamviin wore their skeletons on the outsides of their bodies instead of inside like human beings, porpoises, gorillas, and what-have-you, although, unlike crabs, they wore a thin layer of skin over their exoskeletons.

The remarkable difference, setting them apart from crabs and every other creature which had evolved on Earth, was that they were trilaterally, instead of bilaterally, symmetrical. Cut a human or a chimp down the centerline (a depressing thought, considering the situation Berdan found himself in now), and each half would be a mirror image of the other, whereas a lamviin would have to be cut into thirds.

With humans, almost everything was in pairs: two eyes, two ears, two arms, two legs, and so on. With lamviin, it was trios or triads or whatever they called it: what started out as three stout legs (or arms, with lamviin it was pretty much the same thing) where, crablike, they joined the carapace, wound up as nine smaller appendages by the time they reached the ground, having branched somewhere in the middle, terminating in delicate hands with three opposing fingers.

Or toes.

When Berdan's ancestors had climbed down out of the trees, their next great accomplishment had been getting up off all fours and standing erect. The lamviin feat was walking on just six of their branched limbs, holding the remaining three up in front ("front" being defined as the side on which three limbs were being held up) to use as arms. It didn't matter which three. They were inclined to swap off now and again. Berdan, always fascinated by extraterrestrials, had read somewhere that showing a habitual preference in this regard was considered to be the lamviin equivalent of bad table manners or sloppy posture.

Somewhere, some poor little lamviin's grandfather was hollering about that right now.

He also knew, beneath the rubbery protection of the smartsuit, which the lamviin (imitating almost every other sapient species in the Confederacy) had adopted, this particular specimen, like all other members of its race, would be covered with coarse, medium-length fur, rather like that of a seal, varying in color from individual to individual, and also from the upper portion of each individual's body to the tips of its limbs. All he could see of this one's fur, above and between the three large, equal-spaced eyes set between the legs just at the rim of the carapace, was a golden toasty color, shading to light brown.

It was said lamviin displayed emotions through changes in the texture of their fur. If so, Berdan didn't know how to interpret what this one was feeling. Its fur was straight, flat, and smooth, maybe with a touch of curl at the ends.

Above its eyes at the top of its body, was a wide, three-jawed mouth of a glossy, hornlike substance not unlike the beak of a squid.

Much like a porpoise in this respect, this wasn't where its voice had come from. Lamviin breathed and spoke through six orifices located, two apiece, at the bases of the legs. Berdan had always wondered—although he was too polite to ask now—whether a lamviin could sing along with itself in six-part harmony.

The boy opened his mouth to speak, realized he couldn't think of anything to say, and shut it again.

"To answer just a few of your unspoken questions," the lamviin offered, "you aren't in real peril of your life and never have been, since these hunting johnnies snatched you from the jaws of the can-can. Your possessions are in honest tendrils and will, in due course, be returned to you. You are, at present, in a native village whose name you aren't equipped to pronounce, situated precisely upon Majesty's equator. There are an awe-inspiring six metric miles"—here, the lamviin pointed straight down, with a dramatic flourish of one of its fingers—"from where you and I find ourselves standing right now to the bedrock, genuine—if unexplored and tantalizingly unexplorable—surface of the planet."

Having nothing to say, Berdan said nothing.

"Doubtless," it continued, "you now find yourself speechless, if not at my statistics or with gratitude at my sudden and fortuitous appearance, then certainly in surprise and indignation at this outrage which has been perpetrated upon your person. So was I, when they first did this to me, whereas they—" The traces of curl were gone now from its fur as the lamviin indicated the entire raftlike village around them with all of its inhabitants.

The image came to Berdan's mind (not from his implant but from his imagination) of this overcivilized being flailing around, crablike, in the taflak boiling pot, and he had to suppress a snicker. Did lamviin turn red when they were cooked?

"They all think it's bloody marvelous, frightening the tourists out of their wits, so they'll flock back to watch their friends being frightened the next time."

"You mean—" Berdan, just becoming aware he was dripping wet, had managed to produce two words. Part of the problem was that all of this was beginning to strike him as funny.

"Precisely, my dear fellow. It's their idea of a joke."

"*Grrr!*"

It hadn't been a real growl but something halfway between a tooth-chattering shiver and laughter suppressed, not just for the sake of the lamviin's feelings, but because Berdan was afraid it was the beginning of hysteria.

"My sentiments"—the lamviin had misunderstood the noise Berdan had made—"exactly." It sighed.

"On the other hand, I suppose, these things are culturally relative. Some people are tone-deaf, some are color-blind, and, then again, especially in the view of the taflak, who fancy themselves colossal jokesters, half the universe is humor-numb."

"Humor-numb?" Berdan repeated the odd word. If his not-quite-growl were to be counted, it was his fourth so far. "You're telling me these people think we Confederates don't have a funnybone?"

"Funnybone?" It was the same tone Berdan used for "humor-numb."

Its fur acquiring a slight spiky texture, which the boy interpreted, correct or not, as a worried look, the lamviin extracted from its pouch a hand-sized object which, although triangular in shape, opened at one corner and had pages which could be leafed through. Berdan suspected it was a language dictionary, something on the order of: *English-Lamviin, Lamviin-English, Featuring Over 6000 Handy Phrases, and a Guide to Confederate Weights and Measures.*

"There's a new one," the lamviin muttered to itself. "Let me see: 'funnybone,' 'funnybone'…dashed difficult to turn the pages when one's fingers are stiff with the cold. I wonder if it mightn't be a cognate to something Latin—ah!"

It put the phrasebook away.

"Precisely, my dear fellow, the taflak believe—and of course in my case they're quite literally correct—that we of the Confederacy lack a humerus."

"Well…" Berdan grinned—it was a painful expression under the circumstances—still straining to hold back what he feared might turn out to be insane laughter. As a distraction, he looked around at the taflak who were looking back at him. He was beginning to notice some individual variations among them now, differences in size, plumpness, hair texture, and in their coloring, which ranged from a light slate gray, through various shades of blue, to purple-black. Whether this denoted age or gender or what, he wasn't prepared to guess.

"They don't," he suggested, "seem to have much in the way of bones of any kind, if you ask me."

"Hmmm."

Berdan couldn't be aware that the lamviin was regarding him with a curious expression, nor that, with its eyes arranged they way they were, it didn't need to move its head—its body—to follow the boy's gaze around the village. Either this young human was most resilient or the storm had yet to break.

Berdan shrugged—a cold, wet, squishy gesture—and it was this and a certain amount of relief after twice thinking he'd been about to die a horrible death, rather than the lamviin's weak puns or quizzical expression, that broke his self-control.

He chuckled, caught himself with a hand over his mouth, and chuckled again.

It was like an uncontrollable fit of hiccups. He looked from the dozens of taflak surrounding them, to the lamviin in its odd getup, to the oversized cooking pot behind him, down at himself (grass-stained and soggy), and began to laugh, collapsing against the pot—still cold, since the fire had just lasted a few seconds—until he couldn't breathe and tears were streaming from his eyes.

Once opened, the doors to hysteria couldn't be closed again, and it began to spread. Before he knew it, the lamviin had collapsed beside him, its fur curled tight, its leg-nostrils making peculiar hooting noises and wheezes, independent of one another.

He'd bet lamviin *could* sing in harmony with themselves, Berdan thought, and the idea—like everything else at the moment—seemed too hilarious for words. It started him laughing all over again, until he thought he'd suffocate. He put one arm around the creature as they both convulsed with laughter.

It, too, had tears in its eyes.

All three of them.

The taflak, hundreds of them now, closed in around the laughing pair, their whistling louder and higher-pitched than ever. The whole silly thing, Berdan thought, had been some kind of ritual ordeal, a ceremony, a test. They liked somebody who could take a joke, and in all probability ate anybody who couldn't.

One of them—one of Berdan's original rescuers or captors, he thought—slapped him on the back with a fuzzy tentacle. If a slap can be tentative, this one was. The taflak seemed to stand back, waiting to see the boy's reaction to the gesture.

For his part, Berdan, more helpless now than he'd ever been out on the Sea of Leaves, seized the tentacle, pulled against the native for support and went on laughing.

Despite himself—and despite the peculiar and scary circumstances—he was beginning to like this fellow Pemot.

All right, *and* the taflak, as well.

Chapter IX

Marooned

"...**a**nd the word 'cannibal,'" Pemot insisted, "wouldn't have been a correct technical description in any case. Unless you insist upon taking the Pan-sapient position that all intelligent lifeforms are members, ethically, of the same species."

Somewhat resembling an octopus on a beach ball, with his legs draped all around its circumference, the lamviin rocked back on the inflatable hassock which served his kind as a camping stool. Not far away, in a small ceramic holder with a perforated cover, burned a stick of *kood*, a gentle incense which seemed to energize and relax him, in the same way a cup of tea might for a human being.

"Mmph." Berdan replied from around a bite of his Sodde Lydfan sandshrimp sandwich, "It's not a bad way to look at things, is it?"

"No." Pemot leaned over and inhaled the *kood* smoke. "No, I suppose it isn't, at that."

Night had fallen over the Sea of Leaves.

Following the taflaks' practical joke "ceremony" and a resulting outburst of hysterical laughter which had ended, for Berdan, in a deep and dreamless sleep (the boy had been carried again, this time unconscious, to this hive-shaped hut which the taflak had loaned Pemot), he'd recovered his belongings—his own zippered Kevlar bag and his father's gun case—and had discovered among the Sodde Lydfan's rations several items he could stack together into a makeshift meal.

While he ate—at his side where he sat on the floor was a small folding cup from his father's belt, now filled with rainwater, since lamviin, being evolved from desert creatures, seldom drink liquids—Pemot had been explaining to the boy what he was doing on the planet Majesty.

"These equatorial folk aren't the first to have thought up the cannibal joke, you see."

"Some joke!" Berdan munched his sandwich and went on listening, although for a different sort of information than Pemot might have suspected. The boy hadn't yet decided whether to tell the lamviin what had brought him down to the surface of the planet.

"They seem," Pemot continued, "to have heard about it from neighboring tribes, who, in their turn, heard about it from others. Invariably these neighbors are further north, as long as we're talking about the northern hemisphere of Majesty, or further south when we're talking about the southern hemisphere. The joke therefore seems to have originated somewhere around the poles."

"Wouldn't know anything about that." Berdan grinned. "I'm Bohemian, myself."

"Yes?" Pemot didn't seem to get it. Instead, he pulled another triangle-shaped book out of his pocket, flipped it open, jotted down a brief note, and put it away.

"In any event, these people we're staying with hadn't worked the joke before—although they'd gone to enormous lengths just preparing for it—and were anxious to try it out. Taken altogether, it was something that I, as the galaxy's only taflakologist, felt was something worth taking time to investigate."

"Why?"

"Because, my dear fellow, nobody seems to know where jokes come from in any civilization. They simply pop up one day and—but here was perhaps this planet's first successful practical joke, being spread far and wide by what we call the 'folk process'—"

"I see, sort of a folk joke."

"Isn't that what I—oh. Another attempt to demonstrate that you've a humerus?"

"Why not? It seems to have worked with the taflak. What did you do when they threw you in that gigantic pot?"

"That was different. In the first place, the climate here is much too cold for me, and I rather enjoyed the unexpected warmth, however damp the experience. My people, as you may be aware, have a considerable aversion to water. Also, it was what I was here to investigate. I pretended to go along, although I confess, it didn't really strike me as funny until I saw it played on you."

Berdan snorted. "Isn't that the point?"

"Why, I—" Once again the Sodde Lydfan scholar pulled out his peculiar three-sided notebook and started up furiously scribbling. This time he was at it for a long while. His stick of *kood* burned out. Berdan finished eating, tidied up—the chore amounted to nothing more than stuffing plastic bags into one another and placing them where they could quietly and safely self-destruct—and pushed aside the hand-loomed curtain which covered the door to peer out into the night.

If Majesty possessed a moon, it had either set or wasn't up yet. Outside the hut, village and sea were as dark as Berdan, a city boy, had ever imagined anything could be—like the inside of a closet, he kept thinking, with the door shut tight. His grandfather had punished him that way on more than one occasion: locked him in a closet. It was the stuff many of his nightmares were made of.

Inside, they had more than enough light. His new friend had come equipped for ten taflakological expeditions, and an item he'd scrimped on least was portable fusion-powered lamps. Four were burning now in a space not much larger than the closet which the outdoors reminded the boy of. In addition to the Sodde Lydfan and the human, the hut was jammed with the remainder of Pemot's gear, a great deal of it, Berdan observed, electronic in character.

"You see—" When the lamviin scientist felt he'd written enough, he put his notebook away. "The taflak are a bit more advanced, technologically speaking, than they appear at first blush."

"Oh?"

Still exhausted after his series of ordeals, Berdan wasn't listening—he'd responded out of politeness—but was giving the inside walls of the hut an idle examination. First impressions were mistaken he decided, it wasn't a bit like shredded wheat. More like living in a giant cable-knit sweater someone had stretched and ironed. He didn't have any idea what Pemot was talking about or how they'd gotten to this particular topic. He'd learn that Pemot, preoccupied with his own thoughts and sometimes absent-minded, often started conversations in the middle. An odd sort of efficiency, it saved time and breath, provided the other fellow could keep up with the sudden changes of subject.

"Quite so. Their potential for development has been limited by their environment."

To Berdan, who caught the tail end, this statement sounded suspicious, like one of his grandfather's many excuses for various personal failures and shortcomings.

He said as much.

"Oh, no," the lamviin protested. "What I meant—well, why do you suppose porpoises, given their undeniable intellectual prowess, never discovered fire on their own?"

Berdan laughed. "Okay, I get it. Hard to light fires underwater."

"You see my point. Our friends the taflak labor under comparable disadvantages, believe me. It's rather difficult to find chipping flint or to mine copper when the nearest solid ground is six miles underfoot. And yet they manage, by various processes, to extract a number of surprisingly sophisticated materials from specialized portions of the single plant species on the planet."

"That's interesting. Such as?"

"Such as that rather large pot with which we both share an intimate acquaintance, the pride and joy of the entire village. It's made from a clay which for some obscure biological purpose the plant life accumulates, and which the taflak concentrate from a certain berry it produces at a certain time of the year."

"They also have some metal—spear points and so on. Or do they trade for that?"

The taflakologist tried to lift his limbs where they joined his body, imitating a human shrug.

"A spot of both..." His tone changed. "Do you know, my friend, what with that cannibal joke and what happened afterward, your sleeping so long, I just realized I've never learned your name."

It was true. Pemot had introduced himself, under a rather memorable set of circumstances, but Berdan, being busy at the time, had failed to return the compliment.

He shook his head. "The name's probably mud, by now, back aboard *T.E.M.*—a family name, guilt by association. The taflak won't have to extract it from berries any more."

He stood, stooping in the low hut, and stretched out a hand to the Sodde Lydfan. "Berdan Geanar, late of the *Tom Edison Maru* by way of good intentions and a malfunctioning Broach: slapstickologist, itinerant incompetent, avoider of the sapient condition, at your service."

Pemot laughed his hooting laugh. "I say, Berdan Geanar, well spoken!"

He extended the middle of his three hands to be shaken.

"I'm most pleased, sir, in the extreme, to make your esteemed acquaintance. And what, if I may venture to inquire, brings you to this chilly garden planet?"

Letting go of the other's three-fingered hand, Berdan hesitated. In so short a time it astonished him, he'd come to like this strange being and was happy not to find himself alone on Majesty. Yet, however badly things had gone so far, he was here for a purpose he intended to fulfill. This meant finding his way back to whatever passed for civilization and not making any more mistakes.

Not trusting the right person would be a big mistake, but trusting the wrong one would be even bigger. Berdan had already run out of faith in coincidences: not that many Confederates had business yet on the whole planet; it was unlikely, but possible, that Pemot was involved in his grandfather's scheme. Claiming to be a taflakologist would be a clever way to stay under cover.

Berdan didn't know it at the time, but he'd stumbled across the hardest question anybody ever faces—whom to trust—and, in so doing, had taken a major step toward growing up.

Could he trust the lamviin?

Should he tell Pemot what had brought him here?

Could he be certain, in advance, whether telling the lamviin (or not telling him—he could, as he'd noted, go wrong *two* ways here) was the right thing to do?

Believing he knew some of the thoughts going through the boy's mind, Pemot waited.

In the end, Berdan made his choice—although he couldn't have said at that time or afterward why he chose the way he did. That kind of deliberate decision-making might come later, after even more growing up. In the meantime, he spent the next half hour telling the sympathetic Sodde Lydfan about his grandfather, about his parents, about A. Hamilton Spoonbender's Museum of Scientific Curiosities (and Friendly Finance Company), and the fabulous Brightsuit.

The lamviin's fur assumed a puzzled texture. "Dear me, I wonder... no, it couldn't be."

"Pemot, what are you talking about?"

"A random thought. What you've said puts me in mind of a small mystery I've encountered, and I was wondering whether there might be a connection. I rather doubt it."

The boy raised his eyebrows. "Try me."

"Well, you'll recall my saying the taflak are rather less primitive than they may appear. I'm inclined to identify with them in this regard. My own people, you see, while more advanced (we'd just begun using—and, I fear, misusing—nuclear fission) when your people discovered us, were still rather backward by comparison to the Confederacy, and we've had a deal of catching up to do."

"And so?"

Pemot turned a hand over, a human-looking gesture which was Sodde Lydfan, as well. "And so, not too very long ago, as an experiment, I determined to introduce the taflak to the benefits of science and undertook construction of a pair of simple amplitude-modulated radios—transmitter and receiver—such as my people began with. I built the receiver first, so as to have something with which to test the transmitter. Imagine my surprise when I discovered someone here on Majesty was already making use of this almost-forgotten technology."

Berdan's shrug was more successful than the lamviin's had been. "Well, why shouldn't they?"

"Because, my friend, in the first place, no one of Confederate origin has used simple electromagnetics, let alone amplitude modulation, for well over a century. Paratronics, employing the same principles as the Thorens Broach, has too many advantages."

"Okay," Berdan suggested, "if it's so simple, couldn't some native genius have invented radio on his own?"

The pair of eyes Berdan could see (the third being around the circumference of Pemot's body) blinked, something the boy would learn to interpret as a nod.

"In the beginning, I suspected as much. But three reasons come to mind to doubt it."

With one hand he indicated a finger of another. "First, the inhabitants of near-polar villages in contact with the Confederacy, being primitive but no more stupid than we are, trade for and use paratronics."

He indicated a second finger. "Second, those not yet in contact lack materials essential to the invention of radio."

Pemot indicated his third and, being a lamviin, his last remaining finger. "Third, the transmissions, while static-filled and difficult to follow—a drawback both of amplitude modulation and this planet's weather—and couched in what I first thought an unreported native language, proved to be encrypted English."

Berdan was startled, "What?"

Another blink. "Precisely. Given my original mission here, I arrived not only with a deal of sensitive recording equipment, but also with a translation mechanism which made child's play of decrypting the signals. I remain uncertain of their significance, but your story does seem to shed some light. See whether you don't agree."

The lamviin rose to rummage through the technological clutter filling most of the hut, gave an exclamation of discovery, and held up a small audio recorder.

"These signals may have come from the other side of the planet, Berdan. I'd no way of determining their places of origin. I regret it was quite impossible to filter out all of the interference or to replace what it obliterated."

He flipped a switch on one edge:

FIRST VOICE: *D.G. transmitting to H.S., D.G. transmitting to... hear me?*

SECOND VOICE: *This is the Voice of the... Seven. Could We avoid hearing you? Why do you broadcast... and in such an elementary scramble pattern?... realize that anyone...*

FIRST VOICE:...*worried about nothing. Not a solitary soul in the Confederacy's employed these frequencies...this modulation for a hundred years.*

SECOND VOICE: *We trust, for your sake, that you are correct in this opinion.*

FIRST VOICE: *And I trust, H.S., that you're not trying to threaten me. After all, I'm here in person at your insistence. I have a place to stay where I can be reached...although why we had to rendezvous on this...mudball, instead of beyond...borders, where you're in control and it's safer, I'll...*

SECOND VOICE: *And We are here...as promised to make final arrangements to accept the...in return for the lucrative reward you have negotiated with Us.*

FIRST VOICE: *...I wish to speak...again of that 'lucrative reward' you...to. H.S., do you...imagine that I planned...years...contrived the sacrifice of my own...and blood, defrauded...altered their... results, made...appear less successful...and dangerous than it was, in fact, merely to accept a...?*

SECOND VOICE: *...had a bargain...contract. It...taken you... find a market willing...for what you stole and killed for. You established contact...the Hooded...not We with you, and only as a...when you had... no one else. Think hard, human: everything toward...you have been striving in a series of...coldly...ulated steps—gone—if...allow...greed to bungle it...you now.*

Here, the transmission was overwhelmed by static.

Pemot switched off the recorder and put it away.

"I'm ashamed to admit it," Berdan murmured, "but I'm sure that was my grandfather's voice."

Pemot's fur drooped, indicating the mood he shared with his human companion.

"If you don't mind my asking," inquired the lamviin after a while, "why did you reject the notion of seeking help, if not from the starship's security people, from your employer, who sounds like a decent person or your new friends at the museum?"

80

"Because I couldn't prove anything. Because it would have been a kid's word against an adult's, and, no matter where you come from, you should know how that works—or maybe you don't. Because nobody would have believed me, Pemot. Anyway, the whole thing was about my family, so I decided it was up to me. Unfortunately, I was just a tad late, and I had the rotten luck to choose a malfunctioning Broach."

"I see. Has it occurred to you your grandfather might have taken certain measures to assure he wasn't pursued, once his act of theft had been discovered?"

A light dawned in Berdan's eyes. "What do you mean?"

Before he spoke again, a deep breath whistled through the lamviin's half dozen nostrils. "Well, insofar as I understand it, and I assure you that I'm no technician, the Broach itself—a man-made hole in the very fabric of space-time—is a simple device, reliable, difficult to tamper with, and almost invariably functions perfectly."

The boy's chuckle was grim. "Yeah, well if that were true, I wouldn't be here to give you an argument about it."

Pemot blinked. "Indeed. On the other hand, measures sufficient to preclude pursuit might involve something no more complicated than reprogramming an implant-receptive computer, changing a Broach's paratronic characteristics a microscopic amount—which, of course, would throw its calibration off by thousands of miles."

Berdan nodded and blinked at his friend. "I get it—or it got me—and my grandfather used to be a Broach technician."

Pemot began to blink, changed his mind and tipped his entire body first down and then up. "Anyone attempting to follow his illicit rendezvous via commercial Broach, would, upon requesting any destination with one Dalmeon Geanar in mind, find himself stranded in the most primitive area of an already primitive world, a hemisphere from where he had intended to be, alone and friendless. With any luck—if your grandfather refrained from interfering with other traffic—a considerable time might pass before the sabotage could be detected."

"Which shoots down the idea of rescue. I figured they'd be spraying folks to the wrong destination all over this crummy planet, and a full-scale search would be on."

"Not," replied the lamviin, "if your grandfather was at all clever."

"And so here I am. Stuck."

"Quite so, my friend, albeit as a highly probable result of your grandfather's treachery, rather than by bad luck or any incompetence on your own part. I doubt whether he realized he'd be stranding his own grandson. And yet, knowing what you know, you remain the one individual in a position, however hopeless it may be, to interfere with his betrayal of the Confederacy."

"What do you mean?"

"That 'the Hooded Seven' is a name for a conspiracy not entirely unknown among the lamviin."

"Oh yeah?"

"Er, 'yeah.' And that it represents the greatest threat to civilization as we know it."

Chapter X:

ONE LAM'S FAMILY

Pemot's words failed to produce the full dramatic effect he might have expected on Berdan.

Instead, the boy arose from where he'd been sitting cross-legged on the floor of the primitive hut, half-muttered some remark about his metabolic processes—which the lamviin being of a species which had evolved in perhaps the driest deserts in the known galaxy couldn't comprehend altogether in any case and dismissed as peculiar to Earthians—pushed the door curtain aside, and left.

Outside, it was still as dark as it had been, and the village platform was deserted.

This suited Berdan. He didn't want to see anybody, anyway. He knew he must somehow live with what he'd just learned if he were going to grow up at all, but how, he asked the stars twinkling overhead, how do you adjust to the fact your own grandfather's a criminal, a thief, a murderer, a traitor? How do you accept the fact the man you'd lived with all your life (even if you'd never liked him much) had killed your mother and your father—his own son—for money?

By increments, his tear-filled eyes adjusted to the starlight and to a faint fluorescent glow emanating from the Sea of Leaves. Between Pemot's temporary dwelling and the next one in line, he found a shadowed aisle leading to the edge of the village platform. Here he sat down, somewhat stiff, leaning back against the woven wall of the lamviin's hut, trying to think, but not knowing where to begin.

Berdan hadn't learned yet: sometimes it isn't necessary to begin all at once. Sometimes just sitting in the quiet darkness does as much for someone in pain and confusion as any train of logic or course in therapy. Berdan sat, watching the night, smelling the sea on the soft, alien breeze, feeling things.

Before long, Pemot was beside him.

Something else the boy didn't know: the edge of the village platform could be a dangerous place at night—can-cans were the least of such dangers—which was why the taflak were all tucked safe into their huts, dreaming whatever dreams they dreamed. The lamviin, however, although not much older than Berdan in terms of his own culture, was wise enough not to lecture, but just to keep an eye on the boy and on the sea, his pistol unobtrusive but ready.

Time passed. After enough of it, the boy turned to the Sodde Lydfan scientist. "Pemot, are these Hooded Seven guys really a threat to civilization as we know it?"

Inwardly, the lamviin grinned to himself, once again admiring his new young friend's resilience of character. Outwardly, his fur crinkled, the appropriate overt expression for the emotion, but in the dark this was invisible.

"I thought you'd missed that. Yes, Berdan, some of us lamviin believe so: my family, one member of it in particular. The threat they represent is vague, but, I fear, real. And, somehow, all the more terrible for its vagueness."

The boy strained to see his companion's face in the dark, until he realized it didn't matter. "What do you mean?"

"I…Berdan, I think the best course in the circumstances would be to tell you a story—history, in fact—the full details of which haven't been known to many individuals and never before, to my knowledge, by a human being."

It was Berdan who grinned this time. The Lamviin knew humans well enough to hear it in his voice. "Don't tell me anything you'll regret, Pemot."

The scientist raised a hand. "Don't alarm yourself on that account, my insufficiently-legged friend. Believe me, it's the circumstances of the telling which are regrettable, not the telling itself."

Both beings settled themselves, and the lamviin's voice began to fill the night with pictures.

"My native planet, Sodde Lydfe is, like many another world, primitive or otherwise, divided into numerous nation-states of various sizes and dispositions, the two most powerful and wealthy of which, triarchies both, are the continental Hegemony of Podfet, and my home, the island empire of Great Foddu.

"As one has come to expect with nation-states, Podfet and Great Foddu have, since the dim dust storms of antiquity when the legendary Neoned the Aggressor first discovered and caused the settlement of our island kingdom, perceived themselves to be rivals and potential enemies. Over the centuries, this rivalry's manifested itself in many forms, from struggles over colonies, raw materials, and commercial advantages, to short-lived and furious skirmishes at arms.

"It hadn't, until a decade ago, yet come to open warfare.

"Among the last of a long, unbroken line of individuals responsible for this lasting, if uneasy, peace was a great granduncle of mine on my surmother's side of the family, one Agot Edmoot *Mav*. Although born of an influential and wealthy lineage himself, which might well have afforded him a life of nonproductive leisure, he had, over the course of a longevous and fruitful existence, pursued careers aplenty for any dozen lamviin: soldier, aeronaut, firefighter, inventor, Inquirer Extraordinary for the imperial city of Mathas, our capital. The lifelong bearer of an heroic and terrible wound acquired in the defense of one of our colonial frontiers, he'd even, upon one occasion, been put to court martial—and acquitted, I hasten to add—for mutiny.

"During all this time, however, throughout each of his many and varied adventurings, Uncle Mav had esteemed himself first and foremost as a seeker of scientific truth and general wisdom, in particular within the realm of ethical philosophy. Having begun as an humble, pragmatic, and, in the main, self-taught investigator of life's mysteries, large and small, in the end he attracted the devotion of many younger lamviin of all three genders whom, in angry tones, he refused to let call themselves his students or, even worse, his followers.

"And at last, when he'd become an old lam indeed, with painful, creaking joints and the fur thinning upon his carapace—at a time when a final, cataclysmic conflict between the rival polities threatened inevitable destruction, not only of everything lamviin regard as civilized, but of all life upon Sodde Lydfe itself—he endeavored to make practical use of everything he'd learned, everything he'd himself created, in order to forestall disaster.

"It had long since occurred to Uncle Mav that the impending catastrophe, like most of the military and diplomatic events preceding it, was an affair, not so much between the peoples of the Empire of Great Foddu and the Podfettian Hegemony, as between their respective rulers. He'd come to believe the pathway toward genuine peace lay not in the direction of negotiations between leaders and mutual disarmament (this being, at the time, the avenue most acclaimed and heralded by those of conventional mentality who, sincere or not, professed to love peace and abhor war—one which, as an individual, let alone a former soldier and policeman, he distrusted), but in the severest possible reduction of the power, the importance and prestige of the rulers themselves.

"For uncountable centuries past, the untrammeled exercise of free expression had been a revered tradition, an unquestionable right, and a virtue altogether unique to the kingdom of Great Foddu. Uncle Mav employed what wealth and influence he possessed in the establishment of a powerful broadcasting station whose principal function was to transmit his ideas to the people of our nation-state, and, translated, to those of the Hegemony of Podfet, as well.

"He was, of course, arrested—the strained political circumstances having at last overridden the last of our traditions, rights, and virtues—and imprisoned in exile upon a bleak and lonely islet in the south of Foddu, far from family and friends and from the city he knew and loved so well. Being the sort of person he was, Uncle Mav amused himself by writing and by converting his guards, the entire corps of them, to his philosophical point of view.

"Still, the winds of war blew unabated. The storm they promised would leave our world a lifeless sand heap. The first battle would be the last: in the Ocean of Romm two great fleets were assembling, thousands of vessels, many the largest ever seen in history, overflown by giant flocks of dirigibles. (At the time, neither side possessed heavier-than-air machines. When I first saw the birds of Earth, I understood how humans had learned to fly so easily. Visit Sodde Lydfe, see ours, and you'll know why imitating them seemed a hopeless aspiration.)

"Aboard many of the warships on both sides, intended as weapons of final extremity—which, of course, made their use inevitable—explosive charges had been placed which operated upon the principle of atomic fission. These had been jacketed in what was, for us, a commonplace and convenient material, an alloy of cobalt. Although their inventors didn't know it, and the bombs were rather small ones by comparison with those which cultures upon other planets have constructed, their ignition would create a radioactive poison which would linger in the Sodde Lydfan atmosphere for hundreds of thousands of years.

"The final battle had just begun when an astonishing thing happened. High in the air above both fleets, an impossible, gigantic, gleaming hemisphere materialized. Broadcasting on all frequencies, it ordered hostilities to halt, and, when not obeyed, employed powerful, surgically-precise beams of energy to blast holes through certain of the warships—and only the right ones—destroying the nuclear explosives they carried, allowing their crews time to repair or abandon them, and ending Sodde Lydfe's first and last atomic war.

"Of course your Galactic Confederacy had discovered us. An initial covert survey team had measured the international situation, recorded and translated Uncle Mav's broadcasts. Not certain what to do about it, if anything, they'd sent for the starship *Tom Paine Maru*, which stopped the war (although debate still rages in certain quarters—Confederate, not Sodde Lydfan—whether it was ethical to interfere at all). Aided by his friends and family, a Confederate commando broke Uncle Mav out of prison. Afterward, as the Confederacy's liaison with the Fodduan government and royal family, he helped make the peace—this second chance he'd won for us, all unknowing—a thing of permanence.

"Now I've not inflicted this long and tedious story upon you without a purpose. During the aftermath, certain parties, neither Earthian in origin nor Sodde Lydfan, approached my Uncle Mav on the quiet with a curious proposition. Warning him of hidden imperialistic intentions on the part of the Galactic Confederacy and pointing out—they were correct in this—his own great popularity among all lamviin everywhere on Sodde Lydfe, they offered to place him in unanswerable power over the entire planet and to help it win free of all external interference.

Being far more interested in seeing his philosophical ideals realized—and, remaining the same inveterate seeker of truth he'd been in his youth, desiring, perhaps, to spend the remainder of his life exploring the universe under the aegis of Confederate technology—Uncle Mav rejected the offer, in one of the rare instances of his life when he *initiated* force against another intelligent being. He kicked their lamviin representative down a long flight of stairs, Broached aboard *Tom Paine Maru*, still hanging in orbit above Sodde Lydfe, applied for a position as a common crewlam, and for immediate biomedical rejuvenation.

"Uncle Mav still visits Great Foddu upon occasion, but is otherwise to be found on even newer planets with his own survey team. The point, as I'm sure you've anticipated by now, is that the certain parties who in vain attempted to establish him as their puppet dictator, represented themselves as the Hooded Seven."

Both beings sat silent for a long while, as darkness reclaimed the night around them.

It was the human who spoke at last. "Some coincidence, isn't it?"

Pemot's blink was invisible. "You refer to encountering the Hooded Seven again, here on Majesty? In all truth, Berdan, I confess my greatest fear is that it hasn't been a coincidence at all."

"I see," the boy answered. "You think maybe they have it in for your whole family?"

The lamviin's tone was a startled one. "My word, such a notion hadn't occurred to me at all. Not a pleasant thought, that. No, I'm far more concerned with their presence on this planet as an indication of how widespread their influence must be throughout the galaxy."

Berdan stood up. "Okay, my too-many-legged friend, since you're telling the stories tonight, what do we do about it?"

Pemot thought. "Our primary consideration, of course, is to discuss getting you back to the fleet. I regret to say, where your interests are concerned, I'm effectively—if voluntarily—marooned upon this planet, having had, when I came to this place, specific scientific goals in mind, rather than a timetable, and having made, on that account, no particular arrangements for my return to a more civilized—"

Berdan's jaw dropped, and a look of betrayed astonishment swept over his face. All of this was lost on the lamviin in the darkness, but the boy's tone made up for it.

"Nothing doing! I came here with a specific goal in mind myself—finding a thief and getting some stolen property back—and I'm not leaving until—"

Pemot raised a hand, which he had to place on the boy's shoulder to interrupt the flow of angry words.

"Come, come, Berdan. Let's be realistic. Far be it from me to point out the obvious: you're an immature human—a mere fifteen-year-old boy—pursuing a dangerous and perhaps impossible objective better left to the regular security—"

Berdan shook his head. "Okay, Pemot, if that's the way you feel, I can do without your help. Go ahead with your scientific goals, and I'll get on with what I have to do! Just lay off the fifteen-year-old-immature-human stuff and try to stay out of my way, that's all I ask!"

He set his mouth in a hard line intended to control a trembling lower lip, folded his arms across his chest, and turned his back on the lamviin. A longer silence followed this time, during which each being was busy readjusting his thoughts about the other, one, perhaps, less accurate in this than the other.

Pemot was the first to speak. "I believe, my friend—if I may still call you thus—I may have been misled about your civilization. Aren't all of the most cherished myths of humanity concerned with returning from someplace you didn't want to be: Ulysses and Ithaca, ruby slippers and Kansas, the Shire, back to the future, all of that?"

Berdan was a while replying. "Would we be cross-stitching the galaxy in thousands of starships, many built to stay out forever? Would our stories have been written at all? Haven't you noticed they're all about adventures the hero has while he's away—adventures which would be impossible at home—and they all end when he gets back?"

Pemot lifted his right hand and scratched his carapace just below the jaw.

89

"Or she. No, Berdan, despite the fact I've been calling myself a xenopraxeologist—a scientific observer of sapient beings—for several years (yours or mine, it doesn't matter which), I'm ashamed to say I'd never noticed before. And I've even been to Kansas, a place which no sane being would ever want—"

"One more thing," Berdan interrupted, "even if the idea was getting home, in the stories you can never do it until you've taken care of whatever it was you left home to do."

"Hmmm. Sack Troy, get the Scarecrow a brain, destroy the One Ring, fix up Dad and Mum—I see!"

"Sure," Berdan replied, "it's a long-standing human tradition: 'A man's gotta do what a man's gotta do'—even if it's just a fifteen-year-old kid like me."

"Or a woman or a little girl—it all makes sense now! You aren't so different from us, after all! *Ku sro Eppdonnad'n Ouongadh*, Berdan, a dissertation lurks here, somewhere, and a tenured professorship for me at the University of Mathas! Imagine: Sodde Lydfe is crawling with humans—I beg your pardon, the usage was figurative—and I come all this distance, to a planet alien to both of us, just to learn a vital fact about your species, Berdan, which—"

"One more thing—"

"What? You said 'one more thing' before, Berdan."

"Sorry, Pemot, this is one *more* one-more-thing. Please don't call me Berdan."

"Eh?"

"You heard me..." He raised a clenched fist. "I won't be related to a crook, not anymore. And I don't want to hear the name Berdan Geanar ever again.

"From this moment on, just like my father before me, I'm calling myself MacDougall Bear."

Chapter XI:

The Gossamer Bomber

"Very well, then." Pemot pushed the curtain aside as he and his human companion reentered the hut. "I recognize when I've been vanquished, if not, perhaps, by superior logic, then at least by arguments which satisfy my sense of the fitness of things. That being so, we're obliged to take stock, make plans concerning what we—"

"We?" the boy asked the lamviin. "What's all this 'we' stuff, all of a sudden?"

"And why not, friend Ber—Mac, er, Bear? Am I not also a member, albeit a new one, of the civilization which is threatened by the crime you seek to set to rights? Don't I also have, if not an obligation, then a right to act toward the same end?"

The boy took his place on the floor, this time in a reclining position. Pemot settled onto a large air cushion, substituting for a traditional lamviin sand bed.

"Well, I—"

Pemot threw all three hands in the air. "Of course I do! How can you even question it? It's indubitable that you require my assistance. Whilst I, xenopraxeologist that I am, shall learn as much from you, I assure you, as you'll ever learn from me. Besides, as Uncle Mav's fond of saying, 'the game's afoot!'—you know, I've always wondered what that means."

McDougall Bear yawned. "But what about your taflakological studies?"

"Nearing completion in the first place," the lamviin answered, familiar enough with a human yawn that his own breathing spiracles dilated, "and in the second, given the task which lies before us, by no means to be discontinued in the foreseeable future."

The boy blinked. "What do you mean?"

"Why, my dear fellow, just consider our present soddegraphic, er, geographic position."

"Planetographic."

"As you will—here upon moss-covered Majesty, human and other colonists live in the one place they can, the place we're likeliest to find your gran—er, the criminal we seek, where shuttles and Broaches debark at both poles."

"Okay." Mac yawned again. "I follow you so far."

"You do? I see, another figure of speech. Very well, we, worse fortune, don't happen to be at either of those poles, but at the lowest possible latitude, where the moss is deepest, and even the natives dwell on what one might term artificial islands."

"Seems simple enough."

"Yes, so it may, but correcting the situation won't be quite as simple. Now consider: two nonnative populations have made their separate ways to this planet, and now begin to mingle to a certain degree, the First Wave, pre-Confederate colonists—"

"Yeah—" This time Mac's yawn was prolonged and furious. "I'd heard about them."

"How fortuitous—I do wish you'd stop that, it's quite contagious, you know—and, of course, the much more recent Confederate rediscovery contingent."

Blinking back tears of fatigue, Mac sat up in his earlier, cross-legged position. "Okay, but what does this have to do with us?"

"Well, the First Wave colonists' primitive surface transport, still in use, consists of 'crawlers' with huge balloon tires, powered by work gangs at keel-length cranks."

"The way I heard it"—the boy chuckled—"the First Wave colonists were all cranks."

"Your comedic successes with the taflak have gone to your head, my boy. Where was I? Whereas more modern Confederate hover-craft work quite well on this planet, too."

"That's nice. The point?"

"Am I putting you to sleep? The point, my endoskeletonous young friend, one even I hesitate to put forward, is that before we can avail ourselves of any such transportation, we must first contact either the old colonists or the new. And we possess no means of accomplishing that except walking, Shanks' *watun*, to the poles."

"What?" Mac sat up straight, awake. "You mean in that whole pile of junk of yours, you don't have any telecom equipment?"

The lamviin's furry covering undulated, the Sodde Lydfan equivalent of a shrug. "Why should I have required it? I am, to my certain knowledge, the one representative of my species here at present upon Majesty, as much an alien to most Earthians as are the taflak. Rather more so, I daresay. What's more, I'd planned—and still do, for that matter, thanks to recent events—to be on the move."

The boy leaned forward. "But what if you needed something, Pemot, like your own kind of food or medical help?"

"I've no elaborate requirements. Supplies least of all, having suffered an heroic course of anti-allergic carapacial infusions on Sodde Lydfe before coming—my insides still itch where they can't be scratched, whenever I think about it—and being able to ingest taflak victuals without ill effect."

Mac shook his head, wishing he'd taken similar precautions. To this point, he'd been nibbling on Pemot's civilized supplies and a few things he'd brought from home himself. It might get pretty hungry here on Majesty before this was over.

"At my uncle's advice," the lamviin continued, "I replenished my crop with brand-new, oversized stones—corundum, a trifle expensive, but worth it—before coming here, since this, I anticipated, would constitute the greatest difficulty on a vegetation-covered planet. And were I to experience, say, a medical emergency…well, in the first place, no one within several light years knows how to help me. And, in the second, it is, shall we say, in the nature of lamviin anatomy and physiology that injuries sufficient to injure us are, in most instances, fatal."

"Well," Mac admitted at last, "it sure looks like I owe you an apology. If you don't need something, even a 'com, it's just so much dead weight. In fact, you seem to have thought of everything—unlike a certain party I could name. I guess it's time I started learning things from you, like you suggested."

Pemot lifted a hand and placed it on the boy's shoulder. "Take courage, stout heart, considering the exigencies involved, you seem to have done well enough."

"Compared to what?"

"Well, you've your smartsuit, which will protect you from environmental harm of various kinds and even effect some limited cures, should you happen to fall ill."

"Yeah," he answered, "provided it isn't too old and beat-up to work right."

"We'll burn that bridge when we come to it. You did think to bring a few things in your kit bag."

"You can only go so far"—Mac chuckled, thinking about the haste with which he'd left—"on Lion's Milk bars, Doublejuice gum, and maximum strength Bufferin-9, though."

"And you've your father's pistol—which ought to be considerable comfort."

"If I knew how to work it—don't look at me like that, I never even knew it existed before yesterday."

"Well—" Pemot was astonished to encounter a human being who didn't know how to operate a gun. "We'll see to it, given the first opportunity that presents itself."

"Yeah, well you can start by telling me how it works—and whether or not it's loaded."

"Dear me, I'll give it my best, by all means. What sort of weapon is it, anyway?"

Mac leaned over to snag the briefcase. He opened it and extracted the weapon.

"It says here, right on the barrel: Borchert & Graham, Ltd., Tempe, Ariz., N.A.C.—M247 Five Megawatt Plasma Pistol Rev. 2.3— Before Using Gun Read Warnings in Instruction Manual. Except I didn't find any. What's plasma?"

94

"Someone, my dear fellow, has neglected your education. Plasma's a fourth phase of matter, as in: solid, liquid, gas, *plasma*. I caution you, I'm no physicist. And it seems peculiar to be explaining this to someone born into the culture which taught me and mine, but there you are. Subjected to temperature so extreme even the word no longer means what it did, atoms disassociate—molecules are unable to form—and lose their electrons, acquiring a positive charge which is used, like a handle, to concentrate and direct them.

"Do you, er, follow that?"

Mac didn't answer.

He'd fallen asleep.

Mac pushed the door curtain aside and emerged into the sunlight, where Pemot seemed to be talking to himself.

"Well, that, I believe, does it. I can't take everything, but I never intended—yes?"

"How are we going to travel with all of that?"

Mac pointed to the pile of possessions, as tall as its owner, heaped up on a transparent plastic ground cloth in front of the taflak dwelling Pemot had occupied.

"All of what?" Pemot protested, sounding hurt. "There isn't that much of it, is there?"

Some justice could be seen in the complaints of both sides. The lamviin had managed to compress what had seemed an entire hut full of equipment into just a few large bundles. Pemot reached down to the platform, and pulled a ring. With a loud hissing noise, his belongings rose a few inches from the ground, supported by the hollow plastic boat shape which Mac had mistaken for a tarpaulin.

"It's a sand-sled," Pemot explained, "the basic design being long in use among my people—although this inflatable version represents a new Confederate wrinkle—and if it works on sand, it ought to work even better on moss, don't you think?"

Mac was skeptical.

"Have you actually tried it?"

Together, they went back into the hut, where the boy's bags were still waiting for him and where the lamviin wanted to collect one or two more things, himself.

"Well, no. Thus far it's been possible to hovercraft from village to village, and—" Pemot looked up from his packing. One of the taflak was at the door, and, even to Mac, who knew next to nothing about the fuzzy creatures, it seemed upset and excited. It chirped and whistled at the lamviin while the human boy waited. Pemot's fur began to bristle, and Mac knew it was something serious.

Being trilaterally symmetrical and possessing the faculties of vision and speech in a full, three-hundred-sixty-degree circle about his fur-covered body, the lamviin didn't turn to address Mac, but it was clear his attention had been refocused.

"Something's coming, something they want us to see."

Mac nodded and followed the two aliens through the door.

Outside, it seemed the entire village was straining to look upward and toward the horizon. Mac and Pemot, in identical unconscious gestures, shielded their eyes and peered into the distance but saw nothing. It appeared the single ocular of the taflak was superior either to human or Sodde Lydfan vision.

Then—

"*Ku Emfypriisu Pah*, what do you suppose that is?"

Mac squinted until his eyes watered. He was rewarded with the sight of what at first appeared to be a large, slow-moving bird approaching the village. As it neared, the boy changed his mind. The bird's wings were stationary and transparent, as was its body, once it had come close enough for him to see.

It was an aircraft, silent and transparent.

"It's a museum piece, Pemot, some of your First Wave colonists, coming to pay a visit."

"If so, it would be most unprecedented. I gather the first Majestan colonists left Earth, wishing to have as little to do with other 'races'—insignificant morphological variations within your own species—as possible. Thus they've never associated with—I say, what *are* they about in that contrivance?"

Mac shook his head, and began to laugh. "Why, they're pedaling, Pemot. If I hadn't seen it myself, I wouldn't have believed it. That's why we didn't hear it coming. The plane's powered like a bicycle."

Mac was correct. He and the others could see now that the aircraft's occupants had their feet in stirrups, cranking a long chain which drove a pair of big, transparent, slow-moving propellors at the rear of the machine. As it neared the village, the huge control surfaces tilted, and the aircraft's altitude diminished from the several hundred feet at which it had first been seen to a few dozen.

"Are they planning to visit us?" the lamviin asked. "Where are they going to land that thing?"

"How should I know? It sure looks fragile."

In another few moments, it was over the village.

"I say, *not* First Wavers—those are chimpanzees at the pedals, aren't they? What do you—MacBear!"

Mac shoved Pemot behind the hut. A chill had gone down his spine as he caught a glint of metal.

"Not just at the pedals—they also have guns!"

Mac had just gotten the words out, when the sizzle of plasma pistols filled the air, joined, a fraction of a second later, by the alarmed whistling of hundreds of taflak. This stopped as the aircraft turned and made another pass. This time, in addition to their pistol fire, the pilots dropped flame-topped containers which broke, splashing destruction everywhere. Several of the huts began to burn, along with the platform itself, releasing thick, greasy smoke into the air. The natives were blue streaks, diving off into the concealing Sea of Leaves.

"*Ku sro Fedsudoh Siidyto,* so have we!"

Several ear-shattering reports followed: Pemot had drawn the small weapon he carried, held it with two of his hands against the side of the hut they were hiding behind, and, with the third, fired several times at the muscle-powered aircraft as it made a second turn. Instead of the brilliant balls of plasma the boy had expected, the lamviin was shooting old-fashioned bullets!

Mac didn't wait to see the result, but dived into the lamviin's hut, one of the majority still intact, and went to his briefcase. Snapping it open, he seized the heavy belt, pulled the Borchert & Graham from it, and ran out back to his friend's side.

The flames were spreading.

Several of the larger taflak had returned from the moss surrounding the village, broken out spear throwers, and were hurling slim, deadly projectiles with all their might toward the airplane. To their dismay, their spears were falling short.

"I don't know if this thing'll work, but—" Mac wrapped both hands around the oversized grip, lifted the heavy, tapered barrel into the sky, brought the front sight up between the ears of the rear, and centered them on the aircraft, as yet undamaged by Pemot's return fire.

He pulled the trigger.

Nothing happened.

He turned to the lamviin. "Do you know how to work this thing?"

"I—*yeep! Lad sro mabo al Pah*, point that artillery piece some other direction! Try that lever—no, this one. It looks like a safety to me, or a power switch."

Mac followed Pemot's instructions. What he assumed was a pilot lamp under the rear sight gave off a dull glow. A faint hum could be heard from somewhere inside the mechanism.

Several more chemical-powered gun blasts assaulted the boy's ears. Pemot had at last managed to connect with the aircraft. Small holes had appeared in its forward-mounted control surfaces. Meanwhile, its occupants had stopped shooting, seemed to be having trouble turning or had decided to turn the other way.

Sighting along the barrel, Mac observed, "I'll bet they didn't expect us to defend ourselves!"

A ball of plasma, glaring like a miniature sun and impossible to look at, flashed past them and hit the platform, which burst into flame a few feet away.

Pemot ducked—too late, for the shot had missed him by at least six feet. "Do you call this defending ourselves?"

Mac's hands, wrapped around the pistol, had begun to shake. He took a deep breath—trying not to choke on the smoke which enveloped them—and squeezed the trigger.

A pale beam of reddish light reached out toward the aircraft, followed by a belch. A sickly yellow blob of energy wabbled along the beam and glanced off the plane. Anticlimactic as it was, it was enough. One wing caught fire and began to burn. Its occupants furious at the pedals, the machine turned away from the village, trailing smoke, and sank lower with every few feet of distance it gained.

Both the boy and the lamviin heard it hit the moss with a faint crunch, some distant yelling, and—

"*Yeeeegh!*"

Mac turned to Pemot.

Pemot turned to Mac.

They both spoke at the same time.

"Can-can."

The boy grinned, and, from the texture of the lamviin's fur, guessed Pemot was grinning back. All at once, the lamviin's fur drooped. He examined his pistol and reholstered it.

"Dear me, I'm afraid, in my haste to bring the taflak the benefits of civilization, that I've gone rather too far. I'd forgotten that any radio receiver, unless measures are taken to prevent it, is also a radio transmitter."

Watching Pemot, Mac remembered to switch the Borchert & Graham off. He slid it into its holster—a little surprised to discover he'd brought the entire rig with him—then shrugging, slung the belt around his waist and, with some initial clumsiness, fastened the buckle. He felt as if he'd gained twenty pounds.

"And somebody homed in on it?"

"I believe so." The lamviin blinked. "And because peace has reigned upon Majesty since the taflak, long ago, demonstrated to the First Wave that they may not be attacked with impunity, somebody who in all probability doesn't want us to pursue Dalmeon Geanar."

"Somebody," Mac offered, "whose name we won't mention, but whose middle initials are the Hooded Seven?"

Chapter XII:

Middlε C

T he plasma gun and firebomb attack on the taflak village didn't delay Mac and Pemot long.

They'd already been prepared to go, for the most part, and their belongings were undamaged by the ill-fated and futile aerial assault. Also, they felt the sooner they left, the safer the Majestan friends they left behind would be. Since he understood the language, Pemot took care of the farewells.

These, given the nature of their hosts, were somewhat lengthy. The taflak, like many sapients at a similar point of development, tended to hold ceremonies on any excuse. Mac made good use of the time, however, since, at some point during the battle, his subconscious mind had put his previous experience in the moss together with the sight of Pemot's sand-sled, and given birth to an idea.

Receiving permission from the lamviin, he spent the hour Pemot was away fussing with sheet plastic and plastic-covered wire. Soon, wearing the "moss-shoes" he'd "invented," with his father's pistol heavy about his waist, his bags consolidated and strapped onto his back by the handle straps, Mac preceded the lamviin down the ramp and was about to step off into—or, he hoped, onto—the moss, when a whistle shrilled behind them, and Pemot touched the boy on the arm.

"A moment, if you please, MacBear."

The abbreviated name seemed to have stuck, at least in the lamviin's vocabulary. This suited Mac well enough—as did the delay Pemot had requested of him. The boy didn't altogether trust his invention and wasn't anxious to try it out. Shrugging, he shuffled his feet around one another until he could see what this latest delay was all about. As he did, a large taflak form came hurtling toward them down the ramp, tentacle-over-tentacle, as usual passing its spear thrower and bundle of spears to itself in a blur of motion.

The taflak screeched to a halt and had a brief ear-splitting conversation with the lamviin.

"This is—well, let's call him 'Middle C,' shall we? Nothing like his real name, of course. He and his, er, brother were the ones who first found you."

"And rescued me from the can-can."

Mac shuddered, thinking about the pair of chimpanzees who'd gone down in the muscle-powered airplane. He looked down at his moss-shoes. They seemed ridiculous, and he wished he'd spent the time learning more about the plasma gun.

"Tell him I'm much obliged."

"Indeed, I shall."

When Pemot had finished with the translation, Mac stretched out a hand to the taflak. Thanks to the existence of an identical custom he'd learned from the Sodde Lydfan scientist, Middle C transferred the spears he carried to his free tentacle and returned the honor, along with an enthusiastic whistle.

Given the awkward position he'd been carried in, the excitement at the practical-joke boiling pot, followed by his exhausted collapse, last night's talk with Pemot in the darkness, and the surface-to-air battle this morning, Mac was enjoying his first real chance to inspect one of the aliens—no, he corrected himself, he and Pemot were the aliens here on Majesty—at rest and up close.

"At rest" was the more important of the two considerations, for, left to themselves, the taflak were seldom found in such a state. They were, most often, a blur of motion, and their preferred method of travel was the one Mac had already observed, cartwheeling from tentacle to tentacle, which may have been the only kind of travel that made sense on the surface of the Sea of Leaves and a great way to get around, but made the taflak difficult to examine in any detail.

Just as mankind's remote ancestors (typified by starfish or sea urchins) had been constructed on a five-sided plan, from which bilaterality had later evolved, these creatures displayed an underlying trilateral symmetry, but had, in recent geological history, begun evolving into something approaching the human arrangement. In this rare, motionless state, they tended to balance on one of their three appendages, each resembling a woolly but close-trimmed splay-tipped elephant's trunk, with the other two, used for manipulation, stretched out and upward, making the entire creature look something like a round-bellied letter Y.

The great transparent taflak eye, transfixing the entire creature, could see backward, forward, and to all sides at once—a biological necessity on the perilous planet. Being large and symmetrical, Mac had already seen it, although he'd missed the faint lace-work of blood vessels (at least he thought that was what they were), thin nervous and supportive connections visible through its ultra-transparent fluid between the black-surfaced ball floating in the center, constituting pupil, retina, and brain, the velvety surrounding flesh, the three peripheral tentacles, and the vital organs contained in their bases.

Where the high-pitched whistling and chirping talk came from, Mac never did discover.

"You know, I realize we both took the community joke like real sports and all, but it's nice of Middle C," the boy commented to Pemot, "to come see us off this way."

The lamviin's fur crinkled, the equivalent, Mac had begun to learn, of a chuckle. "On the contrary, my young conclusion-jumping friend, the fellow intends to accompany us on our trek. And let me tell you, I, for one, am most grateful."

More pleased than surprised, Mac peered from the lamviin to the taflak and back again. "Oh yeah? How come?"

"You know, MacBear, I seem to be learning a different dialect of English from you than my professors thought to expose me to in Mexico City. His brother—I suppose it must be the closest equivalent, after all—let's call him B-flat and utter the name with reverence, is dead, most cruelly incinerated while attempting to rescue his, Middle C's, that is, lifemate and, er, children."

With a grim expression on his face, the boy nodded. The moral debt being piled up to his grandfather's account was beginning to look unmanageable to a young man who believed he was obliged, one way or another, name change or not, to pay it. Now add another handful of lives. What Mac wanted to do, all of a sudden, was cry.

Instead, he spoke. "And he wants to go with us and get whoever's responsible for this—this—"

"It's most interesting"—Pemot blinked—"how universal such a sentiment turns out to be. I wonder whether revenge, instead of being the moral error so many claim it to be, actually possesses some evolutionary important survival value."

As Mac was growing accustomed to seeing him do, the lamviin plunged a hand into a pocket, extracted his triangular notebook, jotted down a few symbols, and replaced it.

Pemot went on. "In any event, you're quite correct: while his people repair the fire and other damage—for which, generously, considering how primitive they're supposed to be, they don't hold us responsible—Middle C, here, will journey with us, wherever, as he so charmingly puts it, our search for justice takes us."

Buried, Mac thought, but not too deep, in a bundle on the lamviin's sand-sled, was their portable "justice detector": the simple radio receiver Pemot had built, filtered, and shielded now against accidental emissions, and equipped with a directional loop antenna. They'd strike out for the north pole, they'd decided, hoping to run into a First Wave crawler or a Second Wave hoverbuggy which might save them part of the otherwise epic journey. But, along the way, they'd attempt to triangulate on the enemy's amplitude-modulated signals.

"Suits me," Mac answered, his terseness hiding his feelings. "The more the merrier."

Without another thought about the risks involved, he stepped off onto the moss. And onto a road, in a figurative sense, which would take him halfway around the planet.

"Onto" turned out to be the right word, after all. Mac's moss-shoes performed even better than he'd expected, although, like the snowshoes they resembled, they were tiring to use at first. They made his ankles and the inside muscles of his legs sore for several days but did their job of distributing his weight over a far greater area, allowing him to stride along right beside his six-footed, eighteen-toed lamviin friend, instead of sinking into the sea.

If Pemot held back for the boy, he never said so.

Of course they both understood—and appreciated—that Middle C was crawling along on his figurative hands and knees, compared to his normal rate of travel.

Early the first day, Middle C advised them both, through Pemot, that they'd be encountering far less dangerous wildlife than might otherwise be the case, just because three of them were traveling together, rather than one or two. The native was too polite, Pemot told Mac, to mention that two of the three were so clumsy on the moss they scared everything away within several square miles.

"Although, given a chance," the lamviin wondered aloud to his human friend, "how well would Middle C do in the Neth, the great central desert of my native Foddu?"

Nevertheless, Middle C scouted ahead, rolling back to his companions when he was certain the territory his friends were about to encounter was safe. Mac thought the taflak might have done that, even in the Majestan equivalent of a city park, just because it must have been boring for him to travel at so slow a march. And, safe or not, he and Pemot kept their own prudent guard up, as well.

As they walked along, and as Mac's legs strengthened, the boy took turns pulling the sand-sled. He practiced whenever he could with the massive Borchert & Graham, adding muscle to his arms—both of them—as well as his legs. Practice was easy and cheap, since, as Pemot showed him, the fusion-powered pistol's fuel was water (once given a full charge from cannisters on the belt, it was much more spectacular in action than it had been against the airplane) and its laser—much better than the crude mechanical sights intended as an emergency backup—told him when he'd hit his target without requiring a shot. After a while, at Pemot's insistence, Middle C told Mac when and where it was safe to do some real shooting. Mac discharged a few plasma bursts at broken limbs and moldy outgrowths to make sure both he and his pistol functioned.

Pemot himself wouldn't shoot, since his supply of slug-and-chemical ammunition was limited.

From time to time they stopped to rest while Pemot assembled his crude radio gear, turned the loop antenna this way and that, and listened for a signal. Unlike any 'com enthusiast Mac had ever seen before, Pemot wore the earphones just above his knees—or elbows, the two joints being much the same among the lamviin—where his species' ears were to be found. They didn't hear the voices again, but on three occasions, Pemot detected what he called a "carrier wave" and made notations on a triangle-gridded map of Majesty.

Days passed, during which nothing else worth noting seemed to happen, and Mac, almost forgetting why they'd started traveling across Majesty in the first place, grew weary of the sameness of the blue sky above and the green Sea of Leaves below—gray and black respectively when it happened to be raining, which was often. The horizon was as flat as that of any ocean, and as featureless. He began to think a person could go insane if he were exposed to enough of this emptiness.

Another thing bothering Mac, although he'd never have admitted it to Pemot, was that the cerebrocortical implant he'd grown up using all his life was as good as dead. While it contained plenty of information—not only about Majesty (most of it incorrect, he'd discovered, or not detailed enough to be useful), but everything else he'd ever recorded and hadn't afterward erased—he hadn't laid in a stock of movies, books, or music suitable for a long, wearisome trip. Not much of what he did have was entertaining or even interesting. No object he could see around him, not even the lamviin's hoard of technology (having come from a far less sophisticated culture), would respond to the device. No information channels operated on Majesty to be received.

Squaring his shoulders, he told himself to be a man. This was just like camping out. Like doing without indoor plumbing (which happened to be the case, although one's smartsuit took care of such things when it worked right). Maybe he could program his implant to teach him the languages of his new friends. Maybe he could learn a new word of his own language every day, from its internal diction-ary. Maybe he could memorize the cube roots through four figures. In any event, he'd either get used to it or put up with it until it was over.

He spent a good deal of time wishing it was over.

Every day, Middle C would wheel ahead out of sight on one of his scouting missions and return with some unlikely-looking wild animal which he'd killed for them to eat. Mac admired the taflak's prowess with the spear thrower and itched to try it out himself, but was too shy to ask. Pemot would prepare the game—anything from slithery nonsapient relatives of the taflak to gigantic insectoids (of which the can-can had been a variety) to Earth birds and small mammals which had found a toehold in the worldwide vegetation—on a metallic-foil fire-resistant section of the surface of his sled.

In the beginning, Mac was reluctant to try the local fare. He didn't enjoy the benefits of allergy treatments such as Pemot had endured. The lamviin assured him his smartsuit, assuming it remained functional, by monitoring his processes and adjusting them, could give him the same protection. When it became necessary to eat—the lamviin's Sodde Lydfan supplies were running low, he hated to deprive his friend of them and had no reason at all to assume they were any safer than the local food—Mac nibbled small amounts of whatever Middle C brought back, and watched himself. As a consequence, he suffered nothing worse than several serious flare-ups of hypochondria.

The struggle to survive—for the most part against utter boredom—tested every resource within the boy who'd no longer call himself Berdan Geanar, though he'd strengthened his resolve by rejecting the name he'd grown up with, the name his traitorous grandfather had imposed on him, and had adopted the same name which his father, under similar circumstances, had. Having nothing else to do as he walked along, whenever he and Pemot weren't talking, he thought about it.

A lot.

At night, it often rained.

Tropical planet or not, Majesty wasn't always a warm and steamy place. It never seemed so to the lamviin, hardy as he was. His species had evolved on a desert planet where a cold snap brought the temperature down to 130 degrees in the shade—and where shade was seldom to be found. Only his smartsuit made life bearable on what was to him an arctic planet. Middle C didn't appear to be bothered by the weather and often hunted at night, leaving the other two alone.

On one cold and miserable night in particular, when they were huddled together for warmth under a plastic shelter half and couldn't sleep, the Sodde Lydfan scientist, worse off but too proud to admit it, attempted to amuse the human boy by telling him something of what he'd learned among the planet's natives.

Middle C had just left to go hunting.

"...and so the taflak believe something more than bedrock lies at the bottom of the sea."

"Oh yeah." Mac began to yawn—and broke it off to shiver. "Like what?"

"Well," Pemot replied, "stories seem to vary from village to village, as folktales have a way of doing, but the gist is always of an ancient culture, one which possessed great magical powers of healing, of locomotion, of flight, perhaps of mass-production (judging by legends of abundance in the Elder Days) but which, as always seems to be the case with the mythology of sapient beings, denied, defied, or defiled the gods and afterward paid the price—extinction. Everything they'd built was swallowed up in the Sea of Leaves."

Mac yawned again, beginning to feel sleepy. One advantage of rooming with a desert-planet sapient: it was as good as carrying central heating with you.

"Hey, pretty neat. Sort of an Atlantis with runaway landscaping instead of ocean water. Do you think any of these legends is worth believing in, Pemot?"

"My dear boy, as I just implied, every race of beings which attains sentience seems, at times, to regret the attainment enough to make up stories like this."

"Yeah, but—"

"Furthermore, how could they know, either about the past or what lies below? They possess no written language—"

"Yeah, but—"

"And no Majestan native—nor colonist of either wave, for that matter—has ever seen to the bottom of the planet's biomass, for the obvious reason of its depths and dangers and because of the leaves' high metallic content, which, while it supplies many necessities of the taflak and constitutes a source of profitable exports for our people, prevents radar and other such penetration."

Mac was silent.

"Aren't you," Pemot inquired, "going to say 'yeah but' again? I'd gotten rather used to it."

Still he received no reply.

Pemot sighed and began wondering why he was having so much trouble sleeping.

He never finished the thought.

When Middle C, having somewhat different physiological requirements and feeling relaxed and fit from the exercise, returned with the rising sun and fresh-killed game, he found his odd companions curled up together sound asleep.

Snoring in seven-part harmony.

Chapter XIII:

The Crankapillar

I t came from the edge of the world.

When they first saw the thing, far away on the hazy green horizon, it resembled, more than anything, a can-can on wheels. At least fifty pairs of fat, oversized, underinflated wheels were rolling, rim to rim, linked by flexible couplings. The thing slithered toward them, as sinuous as one of Middle C's tentacles.

That entity, straining to the uttermost tip of his supporting appendage—the equivalent of standing on his toes—became agitated and at first didn't seem to hear the frantic questions Pemot was asking him. At last he relaxed—although Mac noticed his grip on his spear thrower had tightened, and he'd transferred his ammunition to his other tentacle—stood down, and spoke to the lamviin.

Pemot blinked. "I was afraid of this, although I'd half hoped it would occur as well, a stroke of some sort of luck, although only time will tell whether it's good or evil."

Mac had been standing on tiptoe, one hand resting on the handle of his Borchert & Graham. "What is it?"

Pemot rummaged through the contents of his sand-sled, gave his usual exclamation, and pulled out a long, glass-ended metal cylinder which resembled a telescope only until he pulled the front half away from the back, swinging it outward and around until he held a pair of parallel tubes, connected by a sturdy metal bracket. It was a pair of folding binoculars, Sodde Lydfan style, designed for a creature whose eyes (any two out of three) were placed more than a foot apart.

He peered toward the horizon. "It's an artifact, a vehicle of which I'd heard, and which its First Wave colonial users term a 'crankapillar.' Our tentacular comrade's excited because it's violated tribal boundaries which have been tacitly agreed to for generations."

Mac keyed his implant, reran Middle C's staccato whistling, and was able to make out the names of several unsavory species of Majestan animals, among them, rats. "Okay, then"—he addressed both his companions, wishing he had one of the wrist synthesizers gorillas and chimpanzees used so he could speak to the taflak without help— "what do we do now?"

Middle C must have been paying attention to the conversations between Pemot and Mac, for he didn't wait for the lamviin to translate but launched into speech.

Pemot blinked, his fur in a whorled, spiky arrangement Mac believed indicated worried tension. He handed the binoculars to Mac, who examined the distance between them with skepticism, then turned them on their side and used one tube as a telescope.

"In the first place," Pemot replied, supplementing what Middle C had told him with information of his own, "the situation's rather more complicated than one might suspect."

"I say," Mac replied, imitating Pemot's accent, "that's simply too marvelously splendiferous to hear, old boy. Would you mind awfully telling me why?"

Pemot gave him an odd look. The lamviin now had his triangular notebook out, opened to the page with the gridded radio map. "Because this is it!"

"What?"

"There are, as you know, two signal sources for the amplitude-modulated broadcasts. This is the location where my lines cross for the stronger of the two. The transmitter's somewhere within a few square miles of the spot we're standing upon this minute!"

"Great! And what does Middle C have to say about all this?"

"It would appear, he says, that in finding them we've allowed them to find us. They'll be a long time getting here—if here is where they're headed. They can't be going much over five miles per hour, and they're a long way away."

Mac resisted an urge to crouch down in the leaves. "Do you think they can see us?"

"My friend, these people left your home planet only sixty years ago, in 223 A.L.—1999 by the old reckoning—and, although they've had their cultural ups and downs in the subjective millennia which have passed, for them, since then"—he indicated the instrument in the boy's hands—"I believe they're up to the simple optical technology which binoculars and telescopes require."

It was confusing, Mac thought, even when you understood it. Among other problems, the starship which first brought humans to Majesty had been blown backward a long way in time. Thus, although it seemed paradoxical, the planet was pioneered thousands of years before the very people who did it ever left the Earth. Meanwhile, for the civilization they'd fled, only sixty years or so went by.

He felt a fuzzy tentacle on the back of his hand and passed the lamviin binoculars over to Middle C, who'd become curious about them. The taflak warrior placed both tubes before his single large eye, held them first further away, then closer, made a gesture the boy was certain was a shrug, and passed them back.

Mac laughed. "Did anyone ever tell you, Professor Pemot, that you can be an awful pain sometimes?"

"Why, no," the lamviin replied, "they haven't. Why in the world would they want to do that?"

Through the glass, Mac peered again at the crankapillar, which seemed to have come no closer, and remembered reading about the pioneer women, two centuries earlier, living in sod houses on the western plains of North America, who knew in the morning that by nightfall they'd have company for dinner. He tried not to remember that because of the bleak, flat emptiness of the horizon all around them and of the lives they lived, they sometimes killed themselves.

"Okay, so they can see us. You still haven't answered my question: what do we do?"

"*Wheeall seet oursells, small Ersseean, wheeall rheelass, wheeall dheeseed!*"

Mac swiveled.

He and Pemot both stared at the taflak hunter, who, despite his lack of a face to wear expressions on, somehow managed to look pleased with himself anyway.

Mac muttered, "Well I'll be disintegrated," and obeyed, sitting on Pemot's sand-sled.

"I was going to suggest," the lamviin scientist offered, following the boy's example to the degree his anatomy would permit, "that some immediate deliberation's called for, and that we begin—with some *kood*, or tea in your case—by being very careful."

"*Yeess!*" agreed Middle C.

Only a few minutes had elapsed before the Sodde Lydfan had his ceramic incense burner smoking, and, on a miniature titanium camp stove not much bigger than the boy's fist, a cup of water was beginning to bubble. Mac wondered whether the taflak would try the tea, the *kood*, or somehow shift for himself.

The lamviin leaned over, closed his eyes, and inhaled the aromatic vapors of his native planet. "How pleasant. There's nothing quite like a nice stick of *kood*, I always say. And, as my Uncle Mav's often wont to observe," Pemot explained to Mac, "we'll begin with the obvious, so nothing of possible significance is overlooked."

"Makes sense to me," replied the boy, removing the cup from the burner and dropping some leaves Pemot had recommended into the scalding water. "Go right ahead."

"Very well. Majesty's a lost human colony, one of several hundreds founded during your people's disaster-ridden First Wave of emigration from Earth, which through a scientific failure, misplaced its victims in time as well as in space."

The lamviin began whistling, repeating what he'd just said for the benefit of Middle C.

Mac stood up to observe the progress of the crankapillar they were waiting for.

It didn't seem to have moved.

Having heard about this famous "scientific failure" before, both in history lessons and in various fictional adventure programs aboard *Tom Edison Maru*, he was disinclined to be as serious about it when it came from an alien viewpoint, however scholarly. It was

112

interesting, however, to hear Pemot do the extra talking necessary to explain some of the concepts to a warrior-hunter of a primitive tribe.

When Pemot had finished this second time, the boy tried whistling a tune of his own. *Lost colonies—careless of them, wasn't it?*

The taflak slapped him on the back. Pleased with the boy himself, Pemot let his fur crinkle with a mixture of professorial annoyance and involuntary amusement.

"I suppose one could look at it like that. On the other hand, I'm not altogether certain they'd have cared about the outcome, even if they'd somehow known it in advance, As I'm given to understand, MacBear, times were changing on your planet, and the original First Wavers would have done anything at all to leave."

Mac glanced at the horizon—the crankapillar seemed to have disappeared—realizing it had only dropped into a slight hollow in the gentle, rolling surface. For a long while it almost seemed they had the Sea of Leaves to themselves once again. He watched the machine emerge from the hollow and continue toward them.

As the lamviin translated for the benefit of Middle C, Mac frowned. He didn't consider Earth, a foreign place to him, to be "his" planet in any way, having grown up in the depths of space, but he didn't want to start an argument about that now. Despite himself, Pemot's version of this story had its interesting points.

"Okay, I'll bite: how do you suppose something like that could have happened?"

"That I can tell you, albeit without any mathematical detail—how am I going to explain it to our Majestan friend, here? Well, there are, as I'm sure you're aware, MacBear, many alternative universes coexisting side by side, places where, for lack of a better expression, historical events have occurred differently—where, for example, we lamviin were permitted to fight our final war uninterrupted."

"Or where," Mac suggested, peering at the horizon again for a glimpse of the approaching colonial vehicle, "Napoleon Bonaparte won the Battle of Waterloo."

"Quite so, and where, in consequence, the language of the Confederacy—provided it sprang into being at all under those circumstances—is French, rather than English."

The lamviin paused here, in an attempt to convey by way of chirps and whistles what he'd been saying to Mac—who could tell Pemot was substituting local references for the events in Earthian and Sodde Lydfan history they'd discussed.

When he'd finished, he turned back to the boy. "Your physicists and mathematicians, naturally enough, suspected this to be the case for rather a long while before it was experimentally confirmed. You see, the existence of alternative universes constitutes a philosophically necessary resolution to certain bothersome contradictions between General Relativity and the quantum theory. I've already gone ahead to explain this point to Middle C."

Mac grinned. "Yeah, I'll just bet you have. Did you tell him we've even begun to explore a few of those universes? That's what Thorens invented the Broach for, after all."

"Actually," the lamviin corrected the boy, "she invented it believing she was producing a faster-than-light starship drive, at the behest of one Ooloorie Eckickeck P'wheet, a porpoise, who was responsible for the theoretical work.

"By the way, I believe, if you'll observe now, that our friends in their absurd machine have made some visible progress. They shouldn't be too much longer."

All three strained for a minute to watch the crankapillar. They settled down again around the sled. Mac had gotten another cup of water to the boil. Out of polite reflex and mild curiosity, he offered his second cup to the taflak, who surprised him by accepting it, placing a number of his tendrils in the liquid—the level began to drop—while leaning into the *kood* smoke to enjoy that as well.

Mac shook his head. "Pemot, how come it always seems you know the history of my people better than I do?"

"Perhaps," the scientist replied, "because I come to it freshly, like any immigrant. In any case, it was neither Thorens nor P'wheet who bungled the First Wave's departure. That had been predicated upon the existence of one alternate universe in particular, different from our own, in which the Big Bang, which begins the life of most continua, either never came about—I've never been clear about this part—or came off considerably less spectacularly."

"I've heard of that"—the boy nodded—"the Little Bang universe. And the word, Pemot, is 'fizzled.'"

The crankapillar had disappeared again, which all three realized meant it was getting nearer.

"'Fizzled,' then—this language never ceases to amaze me. In any case, ducking through it promised that one might get halfway across a given fraction of his own universe, in effect, in less time and without any bothersome Einsteinian problems about the speed of light or Fitzgerald-Lorenz time-dilation."

"So what went wrong?"

The ripple through Pemot's fur represented the Sodde Lydfan equivalent of a shrug. "It seems to have been some difficulty with astrogation. They made it into the Little Bang universe, as planned— a bit, I suppose like maneuvering their spaceships through a large transport Broach—but somehow lost their bearings relative to this universe. When they popped back out, they discovered they'd arrived just about anywhere—or anywhen (I find that to be the most fascinating aspect of the tragedy)—except where and when they'd intended."

Mac shuddered. Put that way, the story sounded too familiar to his own Broach misadventure for comfort.

"And Middle C," he asked the lamviin, "is still following you on all of this?"

A sudden motion in the corner of one eye caught his attention.

Middle C jumped up, as well.

The colonial vehicle, only a few thousand yards away now, had just emerged from behind a billow of leaves and was headed straight for their camp.

"Why, yes," Pemot continued, unperturbed. "He is. I'm rather surprised, but he seems to have grasped the necessary concepts without much difficulty at all. I confess I'd considerably more trouble with it myself at the Royal College of Mathas.

"And now, I believe we'd better make some plans..."

As he and Pemot watched it drawing nearer, Mac's original long-distance assessment of the crankapillar proved correct in all but three or four particulars.

Middle C, by previous arrangement, had long since found some-place to hide under the leaves.

It was comprised, as he'd guessed, of several independent sets of wheels, four to a subchassis like the railroad cars of costume dramas. The wheels were large—seven or eight feet in diameter—manufac-tured from some latexlike secretion of the one plant species on the planet, inflated to the resistance of a firm foam pillow. Each open car was linked to the ones before and behind it, completing a long, semi-rigid structure which could negotiate any terrain.

One thing Mac had missed was that the contraption was wo-ven out of wickerwork—also from the Sea of Leaves—with only the load-bearing portions fabricated from metal, a substance rare on Majesty, since it had to be mined at the poles.

He also observed now the inward-facing benches on each car, each occupied by half a dozen bare-skinned men—something like three hundred, altogether—hunched in rows, staring into one an-other's sweaty faces, all the while laboring over a long, loose-linked crank, which he guessed was geared to the fat wheels.

Mac was seeing his first galley slaves—for that matter, his first slaves of any kind.

He was smelling them, as well, and wishing he weren't. First and foremost, more than anything else he noticed about the machine and its occupants, was the malodorous fog of human sweat and excrement which lapped for hundreds of yards all around it, regardless of wind direction. It made the boy—and he wondered if it was affecting his companion the same way—want to throw up.

Instead, he leaned into Pemot's *kood* smoke, his inhalations deep—and grateful.

Behind each bench, between those who cranked and the soft, oversized wheels, a walkway had been constructed, also of wicker, for an ugly-looking overseer who, with his partner across from him, made sure their car pulled its own weight. They were equipped for the task: plenty of sunburned muscle and short, nasty whips, which they used with frequency and enthusiasm. As they leaned in to encourage the slaves, Mac wondered whether they ever hit each other by accident.

Projecting outboard between each set of wheels, some kind of long-snouted weapons were under control of the overseers. Mac couldn't tell what sort of weapons they were, but they were made of precious metal, scorched around the muzzles.

Only the car at the rear of the assembly was different, having an upswept superstructure—a quarter—or poop-deck—a striped canopy, and a pair of shorter, forward-pointed weapons mounted on swivels at the front edge of the deck, perhaps to discourage mutiny among those who cranked the train along. Mac had expected some complicated arrangement for steering, but was disappointed.

"*Stand where you are!*" A voice from the rear car was distorted by a megaphone.

"*You're under the f-flamers of S.N.R.* Intimidator, *c-commanded by C-captain Tiberius j'Kaimreks of the N-navy of the G-government-in-Exile of the Securitasian National Republic!*"

Chapter XIV:

j'Kaimreks and the Baldies

"*You have our p-permission to c-come aboard!*"

With a horrendous squeaking groan, followed by a leaf-scattering crash, a wicker boarding plank was tipped over the side of the rearmost section of the crankapillar, and fell at Mac and Pemot's feet, coming close to crushing them both.

Overhead, a mixed flock of transplanted Earthian scavenger birds and their membranous native Majestan competitors swooped and wheeled in hopes the ugly smell wafting from the crankapillar meant something nice and decomposed to pounce on.

"*In fact, we m-must insist! Come, come, hesitation is the same as insubordination!*"

Pemot muttered something in his own language which sounded insubordinate to Mac, hadn't hesitated about it, and so, the boy guessed, the relationship didn't work both ways.

Shrugging, the boy sat down on the edge of the plank, removed the makeshift moss-shoes from his feet, and, fighting his reflexive reaction to the odors around him, preceded his friend up onto the quarterdeck of the machine.

The only reason the deck wasn't dirtier was that it had been woven of open wickerwork. Debris tended to drop through, to the benefit of certain creatures who, like the birds and other things overhead, followed the crankapillar about across the Sea of Leaves. Here and there it had become worn or broken, and mended with some black, gluey substance Mac didn't want to know any more about.

They were greeted by the same individual who'd been using the megaphone. His filthy canvas trousers, once white long ago, had been ragged off at the knees. His stiff, high-collared tunic needed cleaning, in particular at the frayed cuffs and where it rubbed against his bearded cheeks. His hair, long and thick, was gathered into several out-thrusting fistfuls and tied with greasy ribbons of conflicting colors. His left hand was shoved into the front of his tunic, as was the business end of a large, wooden-handled weapon of some sort.

Like his vehicle, he could be smelled at some distance.

His feet were bare.

"*Now, we will just—*" He lowered the megaphone and started again. "We will just relieve you of the s-sidearms, if you please—or if you do not please—it is all the same to us. Your existence is justifiable only insofar as you serve."

He stretched out an unwholesome-looking right hand and snapped a dirty-nailed finger.

"My Captain!" replied an overseer. "Hesitation is the same as insubordination!"

To j'Kaimreks' left, the man turned one of the swivel-weapons around and trained it on the boy and the lamviin. A small blue flame flickered near its sooty muzzle, and a hose led from the breech of the thing to a large drum a few feet away.

Even above the myriad of other noxious odors with which the crankapillar seemed to ooze, this martial-looking arrangement reeked of ill-refined and sulfurous kerosene.

Each time the captain or one of his overseers made too sudden a movement, hordes of tiny creatures leaped from their clothing, skittering across the deck for a crack to hide in. The overseers' uniforms were much the same as the captain's, threadbare, bottle-green, and dirty, although it appeared seniority had given the captain the opportunity to accrue a richer, thicker, more elite layer of filth.

For a long, terrible moment, Mac was certain his queasy stomach would embarrass him.

"The sidearm," repeated the captain. "Your existence is justifiable only insofar as—"

Mac gulped bile, blinked back tears of nausea, and answered between gritted teeth. "I don't think so."

"*What?*" The man was wide-eyed with astonishment. "Have we not explained to you that you must obey promptly and without question?"

"Yeah. So I explained to you that I don't think so. In the Galactic Confederacy, insubordination is one of our most popular leisure activities. These flamethrowers of yours are real impressive in their own small way, but they'd make a tempting target for our starship's strategic particle beam weapons." He pointed a thumb upward toward the sky, where *Tom Edison Maru* might still be orbiting, invisible at present, but a brilliant artificial star from dusk to dawn.

"Infrared sighting instruments, you know, and all we have to do is think about wanting them."

This, of course, was a lie on which Pemot and the boy had agreed while waiting for the crankapillar. Yet, if the unwashed, unshaven, and undeodoranted Captain j'Kaimreks knew anything at all about the Confederacy, he'd believe it.

"Besides—" Having practiced enough to gain some confidence with the weapon, Mac patted the handle of the Borchert & Graham five megawatt plasma pistol hanging low along his right thigh. "Before I burned to death, I'd make sure I had company. There's enough power here to reduce this crankapillar of yours, and ten more like it, to a fine white ash. Don't hurt us, we don't hurt you. Do we understand each other, Captain?"

The man with the megaphone looked up at the sky, as if for some visible portent of the *Tom Edison Maru*. He closed his eyes and shuddered, did a turnabout, and grinned, exposing a mouthful of blackened gaps where several of his teeth should have been. Mac had never seen a man with missing teeth before, and for some peculiar reason had to fight his rebellious stomach again.

"Of course we d-do, spaceboy. B-be welcome aboard our humble conveyance. I will have a stool unf-folded if you will honor it with your esteemed fundament. What is that object you have got with you. Is it some kind of mutated spider?"

"This is my friend, Epots Dinnomm *Pemot*, a scientist and a member of the sapient species which calls itself the lamviin, from the Empire of Great Foddu on the planet Sodde Lydfe. We're anxious to

120

depart the Sea of Leaves, and are looking for transportation to Geislinger at the north pole. We're willing to pay for it."

The captain scowled, slamming his bushy, dandruff-laden eyebrows together. "As we will have you to understand, spaceboy, the *Intimidator* is a vehicle of war, a Securitasian crankapillar-of-the-line, and not some common trading scow. We are not for hire, no, not for any amount of money...how much do you got?"

Mac grinned, deciding not to tell the man about the gold coins in his gun belt until he had to.

"Well, Captain j'Kaimreks, it's like this: we don't have any money with us, but we have friends expecting us in Geislinger, who can pay you when we get there—"

"We offer you," Pemot interrupted, "some of our valuable scientific instruments as security."

"*It talks!*"

Astonished, the captain held out his free hand, grubby palm upward, and turned to his overseers. "Look you upon this, my boys! It talks! It bargains with us, offering high-tech barter goods! We would not have believed it if we had not heard it ourselves!"

From a corner of his eye, Mac recognized the impatient stirring in Pemot's hair. "See here, Captain...er—"

"j'Kaimreks," the man supplied, standing as tall as he could manage and shoving his left hand even deeper into his shabby coat. "Captain T-tiberius j'Kaimreks of the S.N.R. *Intimidator* of the N-navy of the G-government-in-Exile of the Securitasian National Republic. Our authority is metaphysically unquestionable."

"It seems to me," Mac whispered, humming through his nose, "that I have heard that song before."

Each time the captain repeated one of these phrases, obvious preprogrammed slogans of some kind, Mac noticed how the slaves—and a few of the overseers, perhaps those promoted out of their ranks—flinched, as if the lessons had been applied with liberal doses of the whip or even electric shock.

Pemot blinked, doing his best to imitate a human nod. The boy noticed the man didn't offer the lamviin his hand to shake, but he hadn't offered it to Mac, either. Given local sanitation standards, this arrangement had suited the boy.

"Pleased to meet you, Captain j'Kaimreks, I'm sure. Now, shall we discuss business?"

The lamviin pointed a finger forward, toward the naked, malodorous men who'd been cranking the Securitasian machine. At that, they were no doubt fortunate to be without clothing, exposed to wind and sun and rain, since it meant less chance to carry around the miniature zoo each of the overseers, as well as their captain, seemed to have acquired. They sat at rest now, streaming with sweat, their chests heaving. It was clear from the displeased expressions of their overseers this was an unwelcome exception to the normal state of affairs.

For Mac's part, he was glad they were all downwind.

"And," Pemot added, "I've been meaning to ask you who these unlucky individuals might be."

Captain j'Kaimreks snorted. "Why, they are merely *f-feebs*. They are of n-no interest t-to gentle—er, men of your distinction. Their breath and bodies are but a tool of our mind."

Mac bent down to the lamviin. "Pemot, I could be wrong about this—I'm pretty concentrated just on not throwing up right now— but have you noticed the same thing I've noticed?"

Looking up at the boy, the lamviin made a thoughtful noise in several of his nostrils, and Mac wondered, not for the first time, whether the smells bothered him, too.

"Well," the lamviin replied, "even after all my years on Earth and among human beings, I'd claim no expertise on human physiognomy, but it would appear to me, MacBear, that none of these unfortunate individuals has any hair on his head."

Mac nodded. "They're bald," the boy stated aloud, his voice rising in volume and pitch as he progressed. "This miserable excuse for a civilization discriminates against bald people! I'll bet they're slaves for no better reason than that!"

"This is not so," the captain insisted. "S-some of our best f-friends are b-baldies. These are *f-f-feebs*, spaceboy! Can n-not you see this for yourself?"

"Excuse the boy, Captain," Pemot interrupted. "He's young, and we're travelers, unaware of all the nuances. What difference exists between baldies and feebs?"

The captain was almost hysterical. "They are *left-handed* b-baldies! The dirtiest, most insidious, lazy, no account, untrustworthy, sneaky vermin which ever drew breath! They cannot help it, they are just built that way, and have got to be c-controlled for their own sake! They have no bargain with authority except to expend their lives in service to it."

"Astounding!" The lamviin scribbled in his notebook as he spoke. "Having left all of the black, brown, yellow, and red human variants behind on Earth thousands of years ago, these pitiable creatures still suffer a chronic necessity to have someone beneath them at the bottom of the social heap."

Mac nodded, "So they found somebody else to pick on."

"'Peck' is the correct word, but you're right. I'm curious as to how many others—red-haired, green-eyed individuals, those who were too tall or too short, too fat or too thin—they exterminated before they got around to these poor 'baldies.'"

"*Left-handed* baldies," Mac reminded him, "and probably convicted of excessive bathing."

"Indeed," the Sodde Lydfan xenopraxeologist answered, his tone and fur texture grim. He held one of his arms up. "Personally, I'm middle-handed, myself."

"Me, too—" Mac grinned "—*and* Bohemian."

"Indeed."

The lamviin addressed the captain. "I fail to understand," Pemot objected, moral outrage discernible in his voice and in the sharp spikes of his fur, "why any of this inlamviinity is necessary."

"That's 'inhumanity,'" Mac whispered.

"Whatever you choose to call it, it's an unnecessary evil. On my own home planet, Captain j'Kaimreks, until the recent perfection of steam engines, we operated oceangoing vessels which had rotating sails. The invention's quite ancient. The sails, you see, were geared to a drive shaft connected to propellors.

"Now, I've had occasion to observe many times that there's more than enough wind out here on the Sea of Leaves to facilitate such a contrivance, so why couldn't you—"

Shock written in his widened eyes and in the sudden paleness of his face, the captain held out his hand, palm toward the lamviin in a desperate, defensive gesture. "S-stop, you! We do not want to hear this! We do not want our officers or c-crew to hear this! When your compliance is not required, you will do nothing, do you hear us?

"Would you come to our world and d-destroy the entire b-basis of our civilization?"

Chapter XV:

The Revolt of the Feebs

"What?" Mac and Pemot had spoken at the same time.

"How c-could you b-be so obtuse?" asked the captain. "If we d-did as you suggest, foul alien c-creature, what would our feebs do? There would be no useful emp-p-ployment for the surplusage of them. They would have to be ah-ah-eliminated."

He peered down at the lamviin. "Do you call this humane?"

Mac looked forward, over row upon row of starving, exhausted, sore-covered feebs, and wondered if some fates weren't in fact worse—and less humane—than death. "Job security," he muttered.

"You're saying—" Pemot ignored Mac and concentrated on the captain. His speech was as deliberate as the boy had ever heard it, slow and distinct. "You're saying that the foundation on which your entire civilization bases itself is involuntary servitude?"

"We did not say this." The captain was a picture of indignant virtue. "On the contrary, extraplanetary indecency, what we have said is that their only reason for being is to do precisely as they are told, whenever they are told."

He glanced from side to side to make sure he wasn't overheard by any of his crew or officers. "Is it not so everywhere?"

"Not where I come from," Mac answered, "unless you take my grandfather's opinions seriously."

"Nor, any longer, upon my own native planet," Pemot added. "Nor was it ever, insofar as careful studies can discern, among the taflak,

125

whose culture I've come to know extremely well and with whom I've been living for the past several—"

An expression of utter revulsion swept across the man's unshaven features. "Taf-what? You mean to say…you mean to look us straight in our face and tell us that you have been living—wallowing—among the snake-eyes? And now, you…you—"

"Misbegotten monster," Pemot supplied.

"Misbegotten monster, now you dirty our deck with your filth-contaminated feet? Why, you miserable, low-living, excremental, belly-crawling, leaf louse-ridden—"

"My turn," Mac interrupted. "Slime-sucking scumballs?"

"Why, I ought to—"

Pemot turned to his friend. "Well, MacBear, if we've accomplished nothing else this morning, at least we've managed to provoke him into speaking in the first person singular for the first time."

Mac opened his mouth but was interrupted by the now purple-faced Captain j'Kaimreks, who'd taken two slow steps forward and lowered his voice by an octave. "We have got a saying, ugly thing, in Securitas that the only good snake-eyes is a dead snake-eyes. Now, we calculate that this saying applies as well to snake-eyes lovers!"

For the first time, he pulled his hand from his tunic—and reached for his weapon.

Mac was faster with the Borchert & Graham.

This time the plasma pistol had a full charge. Five million watts, concentrated into a blinding pinpoint of fury, struck the man in the torso, enveloped him briefly in searing blue-white flames, and hurled him backward across the deck where he fell, a smoking wreckage of a human being. Little was left of him from the belt up.

Meanwhile, Pemot, watching their backs, had drawn and leveled his old-fashioned chemical-powered projectile weapon at the overseer nearest the flamethrower.

"I'd not advise it, sir."

The overseer took one look at the enormous muzzle of the gun—and at the nine-legged monster pointing it at him—and leaped over the rail into the Sea of Leaves.

The other officers followed his example.

Weapon still in hand, the Sodde Lydfan strode forward to a crude plank bridge connecting the aftermost section of the idle crankapillar to the next section ahead of it in line. His companion, meanwhile, somewhat surprised by his own actions, had crossed the deck to examine the smoking remains of the late Captain j'Kaimreks, having first put them out with a bucket of water standing beneath the canopy.

"Some pistol my daddy left me." As Mac muttered to himself, he wondered why he was unable to feel much of anything else at the moment. At least he didn't feel sick to his stomach any more. "Hey, Pemot—take a look what I've got!"

When he looked back, the lamviin—who'd lived for a while in the North American west and knew something of its legendary customs—saw, to his horror, that Mac was holding up the captain's hair as if it were a Comanche trophy.

"You put that down this minute! I greatly fear what all this violence must be doing to your—"

"My poor, tender little psyche? But it's *fake*, Pemot. It's made out of dyed moss! And, come to think of it, didn't you notice? When the captain grabbed for that blunderbuss of his, whatever it was, he did it with his left hand!"

One set of feet on the plank, Pemot paused. "No, MacBear, as a matter of fact, I hadn't noticed. However I did notice his decided stutter which, among you human beings, is sometimes thought to be a symptom of suppressed left-handedness. Captain Tiberius j'Kaimreks was a left-handed baldy. In short, a feeb. Now I suggest you come here and let me show you something."

The boy crossed a diagonal this time and met his friend at the bridging plank. "Like what?"

"I beg you to keep your voice down for the moment. I'm not accustomed to examining people as if they were cattle, and this is embarrassing enough as it is."

The lamviin assumed what Mac was certain were his most formal lecture-hall intonations. "Observe, first of all, that, despite the racket and destruction, none of the slaves aboard this contraption has so much as turned around to see what happened."

Squinting down the line, Mac saw Pemot was correct: not one of the men had moved. "Are they drugged?" he asked.

"Being human, you'd be a better judge of that than I. But recall: 'When compliance is not required, you will do nothing.' That's exactly what they're doing. Nothing. Notice also this first one on the right; take a hard look at his scalp."

Mac stepped forward and, holding his nose, bent down over the unmoving feeb. He was covered with old scars, bruises, and open wounds from the overseer's whip, and had an ugly, puckered empty socket where his left eye should have been.

"Well, I'll be—his head's been shaved!"

"Indeed it has, or chemically depilated, and recently. They won't wash their slaves, they won't wash themselves, but they'll do whatever they must to maintain their illusions. Some feebs, it would appear, are more unequal than others."

"I guess so. It's kind of scary, him sitting there like that, as if we didn't exist."

He addressed the seated figure. "Um, excuse me..."

Mac's lame opener produced no visible result. The feeb didn't seem to be drugged, asleep, or in a trance, but just indifferent. He sat slumped on his bench, facing the crank which had reduced his hands to ground meat, breathing and sweating. His eyes were open, and the look on his face was composed and intelligent.

Overcoming revulsion, Mac bent further and shook the feeb's sunburned shoulder.

Skin peeled away at the boy's touch.

The feeb looked up. "You no officer..." The statement almost amounted to a complaint.

"Meebe you new cap'n? Lost tracka who's cap'n now. My body is but a tool of your mind."

He flinched.

"I will obey promptly and without question."

He flinched again.

"*No!*" Mac's voice was harsh. "I'm not the captain. The captain's dead. There isn't any captain, and won't be, ever again!"

The feeb assumed a hurt expression, sniffed, and a tear began to form in his one good eye. "No cap'n? Who gonna feed us? Who gonna tell us go an' stop? You gonna tell us?"

Once again, he cringed.

"I have no bargain with authority except to expend my life in its service."

"My dear fellow," Pemot put in. "There'll be no one to tell you what to do from now on. You're free, don't you understand what I'm saying. Free to feed yourself, or starve, or to do anything else within your power that you want to do. You're free."

The feeb didn't answer, but turned his eye back to the work-polished crank and sat motionless and dejected. Mac noticed, now, in addition to the overseer's whips and flamethrowers, each car had its own huge, long-handled brake lever.

"I don't think you understand." It was Mac who tried this time, his voice becoming a bit hysterical with the attempt. "Up there in the sky is a great big starship from the Galactic Confederacy. It won't let Securitas or any other nation-state own your body or tell you what to do, ever again. You're free—you don't have to be a slave anymore!"

"No slave in Securitas," the feeb protested. "Slavery against law. It is the splendid opportunity of every individual to make of his life a willing gift to authority."

He grimaced and fell silent.

"I do believe," offered Pemot, "the joy of sudden liberty's pummeled him into insensibility. After all, recall the accident in the Little Bang universe, the shift backward in time. These people—their ancestors, I mean—have been here on this world for thousands of years. For as long as the rest of human history's lasted on Earth. The poor fellow's suffering monumental culture shock."

Mac shook his head. "Pemot," he argued, "something else is going on here. Something worse. You know, when we first saw this machine, I wondered where the steering mechanism was. I just realized it was the captain's megaphone. This thing's steered by voice command, answered by differential braking at each of these cars."

"Is that somehow relevant," inquired Pemot, "to the situation we find ourselves in?"

"Yes. If I'm right about the psychology involved, we won't be taking any ride to the north pole in this machine. Not unless we want to become feeb drivers."

Mac recognized the puzzled expression in Pemot's fur. Look, you scared off all the spark plugs—the overseers. I shot the steering wheel—Captain j'Kaimreks. And now the motor—this slave—doesn't seem enthusiastic at all about being allowed to steer himself. He's a part of the whole machine, Pemot, his existence is justifiable—to him—only insofar as it serves the whole. It's sickening, but that's the way it is."

He turned back to the feeb. "If nobody tells you what to do, are you just going to sit here in the sun and peel to death?"

A long pause followed, during which the feeb appeared to be exerting an enormous mental effort. Mac and Pemot waited until his features became normal again.

"Nah." The feeb sighed. "Officers don' come back, feebs hafta 'lect new officers like b'fore. Hurt head. My only reason for being is to do precisely as I am told."

He flinched, brightened for a moment and smiled.

"New officers choose us new cap'n! We go! His authority is metaphysically unquestionable. My existence is justifiable only insofar as I serve him!"

A final flinch and he fell silent.

Mac straightened and turned away, his stomach not behaving well again, regained the quarterdeck aft, and began a slow descent to the ramped boarding plank.

Following his human friend, Pemot spoke first, his voice subdued and unsteady. "I must say, MacBear, this is a most depressing turn of events. I suppose some social scientist somewhere knows precisely how many times one must repeat a slogan, beginning at what tender age, until it produces a state of voluntary slavery. I daresay even the late Captain j'Kaimreks was, to some extent, a victim of the process."

Mac turned. "You're the only social scientist around here, Pemot. And people worry about physicists!"

Pemot was horrified at his companion's accusation but knew enough to control his reaction. "Nonetheless, my friend, some responsibilities exist in the life of a sapient being that no excuse can justify abrogating. It puts me in mind of an old Fodduan saying: '*Ro gra fins ko vezamoh ytsa mykodsu yn tas gadsru al ys.*'"

Mac looked up from tying on his moss-shoes. "Which means?"

"Idiomatically, 'Anyone requiring persuasion to be free doesn't deserve to be.'"

The boy stood up. "Oh yeah? Well it reminds me of an old Confederate saying."

"Yes?"

"It sure does: 'If voting ever threatened to change anything, they'd outlaw it.'"

"Mmm. Indeed."

They'd just reached Pemot's sand-sled when they saw the screw-maran approaching.

Chapter XVI:

THE SCREWMARAN

Someone once said "small is beautiful."

He was wrong.

There seemed to be no end, Mac thought, to low-grade technology and labor-intensive wonders out here on the Sea of Leaves. The Antimacassarite screwmaran was swifter than the crankapillar—about seven miles an hour to the Securitasian vessel's five—and had been somewhat closer to begin with, having approached unobserved while he and Pemot were preoccupied with the late Captain j'Kaimreks.

The vessel's name, which his implant supplied along with her nationality, was descriptive. The vehicle resembled the shanks of a pair of stubby, steep-threaded wood screws, counterrotating side by side, connected—to continue the nautical terminology the Securitasians had preferred—at her double bow and stern by what, for want of better words, might have been called a flying forecastle and quarterdeck. She was powered by about the same number of slaves as the *Intimidator*, not sitting at their backbreaking labors, but marching for eternity around a set of stair steps cut into the angled sides of her threads.

At once, Mac could see why the screwmaran was faster. She consisted of little more than a pair of giant propellors. No complicated gearing system wasted the energies of her crew by taking them around right angles. Also, her design made more efficient use of their weight and of the stronger muscles of their legs.

132

He didn't doubt for a minute—although with his olfactory capacities overcome by the *Intimidator*, he couldn't tell just yet—that she smelled the same.

Preparing themselves for another confrontation with the First Wave colonists, he and Pemot sat down near the lamviin's sand-sled, waiting for them to arrive.

"You'd think," the boy observed as he and Pemot watched the odd vehicle approaching, "with an advantage like that—"

"An advantage like what?" The lamviin sounded irritable.

"The several thousand years' retroactive head start you told me about. You'd think these colonists should be way ahead of the rest of humanity by now. But they're not, are they? And anyway, what're you so ticked off about?"

"Ticked off? You accuse me of harboring parasites?"

Mac laughed. "I could well believe it—and give myself a close inspection, too—after a few minutes aboard one these machines. No, I'm just wondering what you're so upset about."

The lamviin sighed.

His fur seemed to relax.

"MacBear, my fine unfurry friend, as long as I've been on this planet, I've remained within the confines of Confederate settlements or taflak villages, eschewing the First Wave population. I might offer several excellent reasons, but our most recent exploit's a good example of why I've pursued such a policy."

"Sounds sensible to me. I could tell you don't much like being called a mutated spider."

"Or being compelled, in self-defense, to employ deadly violence. Still, what I've managed to learn of Antimacassarite culture leads me to believe it similar to my own. My greatest fear is that, despite my Uncle Mav's painstaking tutelage, I may be vulnerable to its blandishments. And this unfortunate world, like others settled by the First Wave—much like your own Earth's early history—has always been subject to cyclic collapse. It's seen countless civilizations struggle into being, blossom to maturity, waste their hard-won substance on war or internal conflict, only to pass out of existence."

"Pretty depressing," the boy replied, trying to raise one eyebrow. "Why do you stick around?"

"Because there's something here to learn, I think. Also, I enjoy the company of the indigenous sapients. Majesty's unique, for all its tragedy, differing, at least in Confederate experience, from all previous lost colonies. And, I might add, as a native of Sodde Lydfe, I can appreciate that difference."

Mac nodded. "The taflak."

"Precisely. My native Sodde Lydfe is inhabited by its own sapient population, and, *feu Pah ko sretvoh*, was never discovered by the First Wave. Although its technology's unsophisticated in comparison with yours, it's scientific and progressive, and its relationship with the Confederacy is, for the most part, as an equal."

He sighed again. "The *taflak* haven't been left alone. The planet's first human inhabitants were intolerant, and remain so, as you've seen. Thus the taflak have been required to fight for their existence since the First Wave arrived. Themselves scarcely changing, millennium to millennium, they've witnessed the whole sorry spectacle of human civilization; and in this regard they're far from primitive, for they enjoy many clever and cynical sayings about the follies of humankind."

"It sounds to me," the boy suggested, with a close, observing eye on his friend, "like maybe you're getting a bit cynical about human beings, yourself, Mr. Xenopraxeologist."

The lamviin splayed all three hands, a gesture of denial among Sodde Lydfans. "Humans on this planet, MacBear. Sapients who stubbornly—proudly—remain primitive, even by the standards you or I, with our respective disadvantages, have grown up with. And in a different meaning of the word than applies to the taflak. Humans who were still politically divided, despite their vast and terrible experience, when the Confederacy rediscovered them."

Mac remembered reading about that somewhere, and keyed his implant. Securitas, the nation-state they'd rubbed elbows with already, was, according to the brochure, a stern, paternalistic dictatorship emphasizing discipline and tradition. "But not personal hygiene," Mac murmured aloud.

"What's that?"

"Nothing—just talking to myself."

The other, Antimacassar, was a welfare state, determined to care for its subjects if it had to kill them in the process; a culture, Mac thought, in which his grandfather, dissatisfied with the live-and-let-live Confederacy, might have been happy. It did sound rather like what little he knew of civilization on Sodde Lydfe.

And, in one respect, the rediscovery of Majesty, the arrival of starships and people from the outside galaxy had changed nothing. Both forever-warring political entities still existed, along with their centuries-old rivalries and hatreds.

Mac told Pemot what the implant had to say.

"True enough, as far as it goes," Pemot explained. "But now the First Wavers complain no one cares about the old, important issues anymore. The rulers of Securitas and Antimacassar resent being eclipsed by a new, more vital and productive culture as the First and Second Wave populations begin to mingle."

"Yeah?" Mac pointed at the arriving machine. "Well it looks like it's our turn to mingle, now."

The new moss-negotiating machine hove to, bow to broadside, a few hundred cautious yards from the immobilized crankapillar. Flamethrowers on the screwmaran's flying forecastle were aimed at the Securitasian vessel, their pilot lights flickering. Meanwhile, a detachment of several dozen figures, men and women, armed and uniformed, swarmed down the threads of the screwmaran, stopped in her shadow to tie on moss-shoes identical to those Mac thought he'd invented, and broke into two groups, each headed in separate directions.

The first group, their old-fashioned bayonetted long arms at the ready, jogged toward the crankapillar, running up her boarding plank, moss-shoes and all. Shouting could be heard—not from the dispirited and quiescent feebs, Mac thought—but no shots of any kind were fired, and he assumed the strange vessel had now been claimed by the victorious forces of the nation-state of Antimacassar.

The second and smaller group, consisting of perhaps a dozen individuals (if "individuals," Mac thought, was what you called people all wearing the same clothing), approached the pair of extra-Majestan travelers and their sand-sled at a more leisurely rate, their antique weapons carried across their brass-buttoned chests, and paused a few feet away. The military uniforms of Antimacassar were charcoal gray, and much neater than the bottle green of Securitas.

Mac hoped that, somewhere in the deep sea moss, Middle C was taking this all in.

A tall, attractive, but severe-faced young woman, carrying a flap-holstered pistol, but no long arm, stepped forward, removed her cap, and saluted them. "Good day to you both, gentlebeings, I am Leftenant Commander Goldberry MacRame, Third and Security Officer of the A.L.N. *Compassionate*, a frigate of Her Imperial Kindness' Leafnavy of the Antimacassarite Government-in-Exile. Might I be so intrusive as to inquire whether you are responsible for having disabled this pirate machine, and, if so, whether you accomplished this by yourselves?"

Still at stiff attention, she nonetheless glanced side to side, as if fearful that, in fact, they hadn't done it alone. Where, Mac could tell she was thinking, was the rest of their force hiding? If that's what's bothering her, he thought, she's asked the wrong question: yes, of course she might *inquire*.

"I do believe," Pemot whispered to his companion, "given the somewhat spectacular consequences of your recent diplomatic efforts aboard the *Intimidator*, that I'll do the talking this time, provided you've no objection."

Mac looked down at Pemot, and shrugged.

Pemot blinked, made a throat-clearing noise in his nostrils, and stepped forward. "How do you do, Leftenant Commander. I'm Epots Dinnomm *Pemot*, a lamviin of the planet Sodde Lydfe and of the University of Mexico. This gentlebeing is my associate, Mr. MacDougall Bear, a human being like yourself, late of the starship *Tom Edison Maru*. I'm afraid we are, indeed, responsible for what happened here"—he held up all three arms—"er, single-handedly."

Someone in Supply had failed, Mac thought, to issue Leftenant Commander MacRame a sense of humor. Without so much as a chuckle or a grin at Pemot's joke, she nodded.

"I wonder," she asked, "whether you would mind telling us in some detail how this, er, achievement, came about....But I suspect that both of you would be more comfortable onboard *Compassionate*, and I am certain that my commanding officer will be interested to hear what you have to tell us, as well."

Pemot blinked and tipped his carapace. "Why, this is uncommonly generous of you, Leftenant Commander, most magnanimous indeed. And of course we'd be delighted. We are, as you see, travelers, at somewhat of an inconvenience at the moment, and hoping to obtain transport to Geislinger."

The Leftenant Commander nodded. "I should like very much to be of assistance to you, Doctor Pemot," she replied, "but naturally my commanding officer will have something to say about that."

"That," Pemot answered, tipping his carapace in yet another bow, "is entirely understandable. I assure you, whatever can be contrived will be more than satisfactory."

Mac leaned down and whispered. "She sounds just like you, Herr Doktor Professor Pemot. Polite as all get-out, aren't they?" He looked up at the woman.

She raised a single eyebrow.

"Yes," the lamviin whispered back, "as a matter of fact, they are. Which, unless I miss my guess entirely, means we're in greater danger than ever before."

"I give up." Mac laughed aloud. "I thought you were going soft on me or something."

"Not," the lamviin answered, "bloody likely."

With half of her detachment taking up the rear, they followed the woman back to the screwmaran.

As they made their way across the open space between the two vessels, Pemot towing his sand-sled behind him, a tremendous *whoosh!* and a wave of hot air blasting from the direction of the *Intimidator* almost knocked them off their feet.

At the same time, they heard a hundred-throated cheer from the direction of the *Compassionate*.

The Securitasian vehicle was soon enveloped in flame, with greasy black smoke rising to the overcast above. A column of uniformed Antimacassarites began winding, antlike, from the burning wreckage, some carrying boxes and bundles salvaged from the crankapillar, others towing makeshift wicker rafts of feebs who, without moss-shoes, were helpless to escape even if they'd been motivated to.

Quite a spectacle, Mac thought. Down deep inside, he'd always been fond of fires and explosions but was unaware he shared this vice with the majority of the human race.

Meanwhile, Pemot commented to Leftenant Commander Mac-Rame on "the tragic waste represented by destroying an admittedly slower but perfectly serviceable vehicle."

"Worse luck," the Leftenant Commander complained. "None of us will enjoy any gain from this unhappy ship. Securitasians are useless as prizes unless newly commissioned."

"I get it." Mac's guess was conversational. He'd been impressed, despite himself, with the pretty Antimacassarite officer and had been trying to think of something to say. "Too much work to clean them up?"

"Oh, never fear, boy. We always have plenty of workers available for that."

She indicated the Securitasian feebs being dragged back to the *Compassionate*.

"Usually their own lot. But it is an impossible task for any number of workers. Sometimes I could almost believe they keep their vessels filthy and disease-ridden out of nothing more than a perverse desire to deprive us of our due."

Boy, was it?

They weren't required to climb the screw threads as the military squads had. The guests' entrance to the A.L.N. *Compassionate*, such as it was, consisted of a thirty-foot rope ladder dangling from beneath the flying bridge at the rear of the huge machine. Leftenant Commander MacRame took a closer look at Pemot and made the polite suggestion that a sling be dropped overside for his convenience.

"Thank you, Leftenant Commander, but I doubt whether that will be necessary. You see, my ancestors were quite as arboreal, after their own fashion, as your own."

He winked at his human companion, something the boy had never seen him do before. "Cacti," he whispered, "rather than trees."

He followed one of the Leftenant Commander's dozen soldiers up the ladder with considerable agility—more, in fact, than Mac, following behind him, managed.

Chapter XVII:

The Captain-Mother

The ladder went straight through a trapdoor onto the open command deck of the *Compassionate*.

This was an expanse of wickerwork similar to the equivalent area aboard the *Intimidator*. Mac could see better, now, how the ship worked. As they trudged along the threads, which were woven as well and had been polished until their edges shone from continuous contact with the moss, the slaves came to the aft or larger ends of the giant screws, climbed off, and followed a hanging walkway forward again. No bulge-muscled overseers brandished whips. Instead, if a slave stumbled or hesitated in line, another one behind him shoved him along.

Somehow, Mac thought, this was worse.

It turned out he'd been wrong about the smell aboard the *Compassionate*. No proper Antimacassarite would permit such a travesty. As each slave left the walkway to resume driving the screw threads, he passed under a shower bar which, if it made his footing more difficult and dangerous on his next trip along the stair steps, at least guaranteed him, after a manner of speaking, a clean death.

Aft of the command deck was a large, roofed superstructure with overhanging eaves, a door, and windows—the silica they required must have been every bit as precious on this vegetation-shrouded planet as metal, the boy realized, unless some portion of the sea plants secreted it—into which they were conducted.

"Doctor Pemot of the planet Mexico!" Leftenant Commander MacRame bowed to a figure seated behind a table and indicated the lamviin.

"Mr. MacDougall of the starship *Maru*." Again the leftenant commander bowed.

"Please allow me to present to you our esteemed commanding officer, Captain-Mother b'Mear b'Tehla. Captain-Mother b'Tehla, Doctor Pemot and Mr. MacDougall."

"Bear," Mac corrected.

"Pardon, young man?"

The white-haired old woman they'd been introduced to sat in a wicker rocking chair with a knitted shawl wrapped around her plump shoulders. She appeared to be even further overdue for rejuvenation than his grandfather. She peered at Mac with shrewd, glittering eyes through the thick lenses of bifocal spectacles.

"MacDougall Bear, ma'am—that's my name—of the Confederate starship *Tom Edison Maru*."

The old lady chuckled. "Dearie me. We greatly fear you'll have to be somewhat forgiving of our good leftenant commander's rough-shod and straightforward military manner. Without a doubt, it has its proper place aboard the *Compassionate*, as, indeed, do we all. More-over, any inclination upon her part toward empty courtesy would be a poor substitute, indeed, for her real talents. Now, won't you be seated, Mr. Bear? And what sort of furniture would you find most comfort-able, Doctor Pemot?"

"A stool would do nicely, Captain-Mother b'Tehla, or I can re-main standing in perfect comfort."

"By all means find the good doctor a stool, Goldberry, and have our aide bring tea in, if you will."

"Aye, aye, Captain-Mother."

Spine straight as a ruler, Leftenant Commander MacRame sa-luted, turned on her booted heel, and left the captain-mother's cabin, closing the door behind her.

"Now," asked the captain-mother, "would you be so good as to tell us what it is which brings the pair of you young beings across the course of our *Compassionate*?"

Leaving Middle C and the rest of the taflak out of it, Pemot explained that he was a Confederate social scientist, a xenopraxeologist, studying the planet Majesty, that Mac was his associate (a word with wonderful, flexible meaning, Mac realized), and that they'd somehow missed an appointment to be picked up by hovercraft and taken back to the Confederate settlement at the north pole.

The captain-mother's aide, another young woman, came in with a well-laden tea tray. Balanced atop a small stool, Pemot offered his sincere regrets as a literal nondrinker, but was agreeable to nibbling on some of the small crustless sandwiches which had been brought with the tea.

Mac, meanwhile, discovering he was ravenous, had several of the things, washed down with three cups of tea.

When asked about the Securitasian crankapillar, Pemot told a reasonably straight story about what had happened between them and its captain—again leaving out Middle C.

"Dearie me," asked the captain-mother, "aren't we the busy ones? And admirably quick on the trigger. Do you know, young fellow, we've been pursuing the thrice-cursed *Timmie* and that rascally scoundrel Tiberius j'Kaimreks all over the Sea of Leaves without any luck at all? You are most valiant, and have our full congratulations and felicitations, but we believe we shall miss him."

Pemot muttered something modest.

"What did j'Kaimreks do?" Mac asked, stuffing another sandwich in his mouth.

"The villain is—was, thanks to your good offices—a chronic sacker and burner of Antimacassarite towns, a habit made all the worse and easier for him since in recent years we have taken to dwelling exclusively upon raft villages and craft such as this. But this is a mere peccadillo, compared to the truly heinous offense against all humanity for which, most lately, we have been pursuing him."

Mac raised both eyebrows.

"He was," the captain-mother replied to the gesture, "trafficking—although we hesitate to believe it was at the behest of his government, as uncivilized as they have demonstrated themselves to be at times—trafficking with the...the..."

"The natives?" Pemot had all three eyebrows raised, although the captain-mother couldn't see the one in back.

"Indeed"—her tone was indignant—"in an effort to enlist them in an unwholesome alliance against us."

"How innovative of him." Pemot's tone was neutral.

"The very word for it." Captain-Mother b'Tehla nodded, puckering with distaste. "Although we are certainly glad you have had a word such as that in your mouth instead of us!"

They spoke a while longer about j'Kaimreks.

Meanwhile, Mac had discovered something else. Thanks to the several cups of tea he'd had since dawn, one of his physical requirements had exceeded the capacity of his smartsuit, which, owing to its age and state of repair, had been limited to begin with. Something he couldn't quite define about the current social circumstances made him embarrassed to ask about the *Compassionate*'s sanitary facilities, and he decided to try waiting for a later opportunity.

If he could.

"And so," Pemot explained to their hostess when they'd finished discussing the Securitasians, "we drastically require transportation to Geislinger so that we may be in time to rejoin the interstellar fleet. Is it possible to persuade you, Madam Captain-Mother, to help us or to find someone who can help us?"

"Dearie me."

The captain-mother's wicker chair squeaked as she rocked it back and forth. "We're afraid this does present us with an insurmountable difficulty, for you see, we represent not only Her Kindness alone, but Her Kindness' Government-in-Exile, and for this reason cannot venture anywhere near the poles, doctor."

The lamviin blinked. "Well, I suppose we can make alternative arrangements if we must. We'd planned walking in any case."

He changed the subject with such haste that even Mac, in his current state, noticed it. "Please advise me, Captain-Mother—and I confess I wondered about this with regard to the Securitasian captain, as well—why do you all continue employing the expression 'government-in-exile'? Surely the Galactic Confederacy's never threatened to interfere with the nonaggressive activities of your respective polities. They're chiefly interested in trade and exploration."

Mac also noticed the way Pemot had distanced himself from the Confederacy. The ploy—if ploy it was—seemed to work, as Captain-Mother b'Tehla's answer indicated.

"Perhaps they do not interfere as a collective entity," she argued, "but they certainly do as individuals, whose irresponsible ideas and actions we are helpless to defend ourselves and our comparatively fragile cultures against. As a consequence, even our own young people have begun to ignore us—and with an impunity against sanctions, which the Confederacy has extended to them. This is not the proper manner in which to run a society, and it is the reason we stay out here, upon the Sea of Leaves, where young people can be brought up properly, without distractions, and with some notion of social responsibility."

She went on to tell them about a great fleet which had, since what she termed the "invasion," become a mobile nation, patrolling the Sea of Leaves, converging only in prearranged places at prearranged intervals. Possessing the most limited means of telecommunication—which they regarded as a dangerous liability in any case—the Antimacassarites nevertheless had an accurate idea of the technological capabilities of orbiting spacecraft, and took pains to mask these gatherings from infrared and other kinds of detection.

As the captain-mother explained them to the fascinated xenopraxeologist, their own navigational skills were impressive, considering the primitive implements they used, and they could communicate with other vessels using flag signals, messages sometimes being relayed in this fashion a quarter of the way around the planet.

Mac's discomfort was increasing, and, at the same time, he was becoming annoyed with his companion. This old lady was just like his grandfather, whose sweetness and sunlight could transform themselves into poison and thunderclouds at any moment, in particular when his authority over his grandson was challenged.

Why couldn't Pemot see that?

"Okay then, ma'am, since we have business of our own and no intention of subverting anybody, why don't you just let us off this machine so we can be on our way? It'll get us out of contact with your precious young people that much sooner."

The captain-mother shook her head. "Dearie me. We could never accept the responsibility for so reckless a course. It is dangerous

143

enough upon the Sea of Leaves for the fully armed and mechanized contingent we have here in the *Compassionate*, let alone a pair of relatively helpless strangers to our harsh environment such as yourselves. Why, for the sake of your own safety if for no other, we must insist you stay with us."

"Besides"—Mac stood—"your superiors might want to squeeze information out of us?"

"*MacBear!*"

"Sorry, Pemot, but, as far as this old lady's stock in trade is concerned, you seem to be buying out the store. I'm not. Underneath all the smiles and endearments, she isn't any different from Captain j'Kaimreks. Can't you see that?"

An embarrassed silence descended. The boy didn't dare explain to the lamviin—who, no doubt, was already beginning to think his companion was turning into a paranoid lunatic—that he also suspected the ready availability of the tea and the lack of bathroom facilities, might be another gentle, hidden persuader.

Pemot didn't answer.

"She'd keep us here," Mac added, "using anything, including initiated force, if we weren't armed."

"Well, young man," the captain-mother answered, "as much as we deplore reinforcing your suspicions of us, it may well come to that, although we would much prefer you thought of it in a different light. You are our guests—and gracious guests certainly do not carry lethal weapons into the homes of their hosts."

Mac felt something cold and hard touch the back of his neck like a steel finger. He turned toward the open window overlooking the command deck and discovered he was staring into the age-stained and pitted muzzle of Leftenant Commander MacRame's stubby pistol barrel. At the end of the spiral of rifling, deep inside the chamber, he could even see a large-caliber, hollow-pointed bullet.

He turned back to the captain-mother. "You're really going to be sorry now. Don't you realize the *Tom Edison Maru*—"

"Dearie me," the captain-mother repeated for the dozenth time, "young man, you don't seem to realize your precious starship left off orbiting this planet twenty-four hours ago, and constitutes no threat to us. We keep track of these things, you know. So, despite your ungracious and ungrateful behavior, we believe you will surrender those weapons and remain here as our guests."

Pemot's voice was even. "In that case, Captain-Mother b'Tehla, since you're so fond of having guests, perhaps you wouldn't mind having a few more. Perhaps a few thousand more."

"Might we be so bold as to inquire," inquired the old lady, "what you are referring to?"

"By all means you may ask. But before you do, permit me to answer with a demonstration—"

The Sodde Lydfan leaned forward on his stool toward the open window, pressed two fingers to each of the nostrils beside his upraised major limb, and *whistled!* The glass panes shattered. Both tea mugs on the captain-mother's table went *tink!* as their glazing crazed, although they managed to stay in one piece.

In answer, a blurred projectile whisked up past the astonished leftenant commander through the window and thunked, quivering, into the raftered ceiling.

"Consider this a message, Captain-Mother, terse in content but certainly to the point, from our taflak friend Middle C. He and *his* friends, in fact his own tribe as well as the assembled warriors of several neighboring villages—whose territory you're violating—would greatly appreciate seeing us, alive, uninjured, and uninhibited, back down on the surface immediately."

"Or else," Mac added.

"Quite so," echoed Pemot. "Or else."

No other warriors, of course, existed. This had been one of the strategies worked out with the Majestan native before leaving him for the *Intimidator*. For a while, Mac had wondered—and worried—whether Pemot would remember it.

Captain-Mother b'Tehla's reaction was well worth waiting for. She thought of something to say, opened her mouth, closed it, thought of something else, opened her mouth, and closed it again. In the end, she seemed to find her voice.

"Snake-eye lovers! Ugh! Goldberry, take them anywhere they please but get them out of my sight!"

In ten minutes they found themselves afoot again and almost alone on the Sea of Leaves.

The *Compassionate* had turned and was speeding away at its full seven miles per hour.

Meanwhile, not five hundred yards away, a patch of moss, just beginning to turn brown with death, stirred and trembled as whatever lay beneath it raised itself upward a few inches, all the better to watch the two off-planet travelers.

Chapter XVIII:

Is It Safe?

Dalmeon Geanar was disgusted.

He reached up to a small, softly-illuminated panel just above his vehicle's broad, curving windshield, which even at this inhuman temperature was threatening to fog up, and turned the air conditioner knob the few remaining degrees to its last stop, trying to wring another drop of moisture out of the hot, soggy air. If the open atmosphere of Majesty was intolerable, here, just inches beneath the insulating surface of the leaves, it was a thousand times worse.

Something moist and pallid—the diameter of Geanar's wrist and with altogether too many legs for his peace of mind—slithered along the side window, leaving behind a slimy track and sending chills up the man's already sweaty spine.

The brand-new smartsuit he'd just purchased aboard the *Tom Edison Maru* didn't seem to be doing its job at all—not that he had much familiarity with such things—another failure of technology to provide properly for mankind's needs. It was, he imagined, rather like wearing an Eskimo parka in the Congo basin. Or perhaps what his eyes saw around him overrode what his body felt.

Odd, he reflected, how from the first he'd hated this planet, how it had almost seemed to hate him as well. Back aboard the *Tom Edison Maru*, he'd filled his apartment with plants of every kind, organisms which he'd always seemed to get along with and understand much better than he ever had human beings.

They were the only things in his life which he now regretted having left behind.

Make no mistake about that, though, he thought. He'd left them and everything else, including each of the many failures and humiliations Confederate civilization had imposed upon him, behind. When this miserable, sorry fiasco was over with at last, he was going to find himself some nice, neat, orderly, predictable, terraformed garden planetoid, spend the rest of his natural life in reasonably luxurious contemplation, perhaps even write a book or two of his own as a guide for his fellow men, setting forth the way they ought to live—and never set foot aboard one of those accursed starships ever again.

Behind him in the back seat of the hovercraft, still in its shipping crate, was that artifact of cold, inhuman, and impersonal technology, which with gratifying irony, was going to make all of this possible, make all of his dreams come true. Perhaps, in time, it would allow him to change the revolting state in which all men were forced to live, and they'd come to follow the example he'd set. It was probably immodest to believe this might come to pass within his own lifetime. It would be enough if, after he'd departed from this unreal world, his wisdom lived after him through its recognition by others.

If mankind had been meant to flit promiscuously about the universe in this life, polluting with his presence the untrammeled purity of the stars and of interstellar space, he wouldn't have required machines to do it with, and Frater Jimmy-Earl would have been inspired to mention it in his writings. The heavens must be reserved for beings who existed on a higher plane than mere mundane reality.

Geanar reached for a box of tissues to wipe his face and discovered he'd used the last one.

He'd traveled to this place, out in the middle of nowhere on a dismal, moldy planet which, in itself, was nowhere made manifest, at the behest of an uncivil voice on his radio receiver that claimed to represent interests he wanted to do business with—individuals he'd never encountered face-to-face, who refused to meet him in the discreet comfort of Watner or even in Geislinger or Talisman as he'd desired—only to be confronted with half a dozen shocks all at once, any one of which could have spoiled his entire week all by itself.

In this damp heat, he thought, it was a wonder he hadn't had a coronary or a stroke.

The first shock had been that long, crude, snaky, muscle-powered machine, the Securitasian crankapillar. In the beginning, when from his hiding place just below the surface of the vegetation he'd watched it approaching the appointed place at the appointed time, he'd believed, despite its primitive construction, that it had been sent by the Hooded Seven. He still couldn't bring himself to believe its appearance was a coincidence, and wondered what it meant.

Still believing the *Intimidator* (which he didn't know by name) represented an opportunity he'd dreamed about and wished for all his life, which he'd planned with painstaking care and worked arduously toward for years, he'd watched in open-mouthed horror as the crankapillar picked up a pair of interloping, smartsuited strangers— one human, one alien—who'd subsequently murdered the machine's uniformed commander in a fiery blast of pistol shots and, threatening more of the same, driven off all of the underlings.

There ought to be, he thought, some way of keeping individuals from owning and carrying weapons.

The much larger *Compassionate* had come along and finished the job, its troops reducing the primitive moss machine to nothing more than ashes, smoke, and twinkling coals.

Some of Geanar's initial shock had worn off. Obviously the smartsuited interlopers had been, like himself, agents of the Hooded Seven, settling some dispute of which he, Geanar, wasn't a party—or simply disposing of unwelcome company.

He'd hoped it was the latter, admiring the ruthlessness of moral character which it implied. If this failed to be entirely consistent with the visceral horror he'd experienced watching the death of the Securitasian captain, Geanar didn't notice; at the most fundamental level he agreed with whoever had claimed that a foolish regard for consistency is the hobgoblin of small minds.

The screwmaran was more sophisticated in design and faster, just the sort of thing he'd have expected of his potential business partners, and he felt foolish, having mistaken a crude thing like the crankapil-lar for the machine he was anticipating.

Thus, with excruciating patience, he'd waited hour after hour for those aboard the *Compassionate* to contact him. He'd resisted, although it had been difficult, the urge to adjust and readjust the simple, homebuilt radio transceiver lying on the passenger seat of the hovercraft he'd rented and modified for this trip. Instead, trying to fill the time, he'd prepared a modest, strictly vegetarian meal using the contents of a small paratronic freezer and the compact microwave oven built into the passenger seat dashboard.

Afterward, he'd read once again from his well-tattered, favorite volume, *The Confession of Frater Jimmy-Earl*, the unaffected testa-ment of a humble leguminist who, through his loving labors in the vegetable kingdom, had discovered the great truth of mankind's proper place in the universal scheme of things. Suppressed by un-enlightened forces who couldn't make money on it, the book was rare. Geanar's was the only copy he'd ever seen, stumbled upon by accident one lucky afternoon in his youth. Yet he'd not profane its wisdom by having it encoded for his implant. Never mind that con-centration on the yellowed pages had become a trifle difficult. He knew them all by heart, in any case.

If the hours hadn't flown by, at least they'd passed. All in all, Ge-anar felt he'd been patient, and expected to be rewarded for it. When contact hadn't been immediately forthcoming, still he'd waited. This was the place, all his navigational instruments indicated so, and the word he'd gotten had been that the rendezvous might occur at any time within a twenty-three hour period which comprised day and a night on this misbegotten excuse for a planet.

The worst shock of all, however, had come when Geanar saw the smartsuited interlopers being put off the screwmaran and left be-hind—only to be met a short while later by one of the sickening ver-min who, although they consisted of little more than tentacles and eyeballs, were nevertheless rumored to be the intelligent natives of this world. He'd gotten a clear enough look at them—adjusting the wind-shield for maximum light amplification and magnification—as they'd climbed down the flexible ladder at the aft end of the *Compassionate*.

Incredible!

It was bad enough that one of them—another of those disgusting clumps of soulless hair and leather being treated these days by bleeding-hearted fools as the full equals of human beings—was that pseudo-scientific meddler who'd been eavesdropping on his electromagnetic conversations with the Hooded Seven. When the Voice of the Seven had warned him about that, he'd been a fool himself to hire those simian morons in Watner, instead of doing something about it himself.

He wondered what had ever become of them.

What was truly awful, almost beyond belief, was that the other interloper, co-conspirator with the hideous lamviin and revolting taflak, had been human.

And his own grandson, Berdan!

"*Is it safe?*"

"Hunh!" Geanar was startled by a sudden whisper close beside him which seemed to come from nowhere—until he remembered the radio transceiver lying on the next seat.

"*Is it safe?*"

Geanar leaned over, wrestled with a coiled cord, and keyed the microphone. "What do you mean, 'is it safe'? And why is your output so low? This is inverse-square stuff. Are you further away than before? Are you backing out of this meeting?"

Although it wasn't audible, Geanar somehow sensed an ironic chuckle buried in the reply.

"*We are closer to you than ever before, closer than you would imagine. You would do well, human, to cut your own output to avoid detection. We have reason to believe the source of electromagnetic leakage which you unwisely and unsuccessfully attempted to deal with is within a short distance of your location.*"

"Marvelous," the man replied, "and you're risking everything by telling them the whole story now!"

The voice betrayed irritation. "*We would not have called had we detected the leakage at the present moment. We ask you to observe. See whether it is likely the source will soon be operating again.*"

"All right," Geanar muttered, "hold on."

He set the microphone aside and powered up his vehicle. Unlike earlier machines of its type, it had no ducted fan or any other moving parts. A light touch on the feed controls of the fusion-electric hover-craft set torrents of air in motion through its electrostatic impellers and raised the top two inches of its windshield above the general level of the leaves. On arriving at this spot, Geanar had cut and attached foliage all over the vehicle to disguise it. He adjusted the windshield for the current distance and light conditions.

Not far away, his grandson and one of the aliens seemed to be busy with camp chores. They were several yards from the alien's sled-like contraption where Geanar presumed the creature kept its radio equipment. No sign of an antenna.

Leaving his machine computer-controlled and hovering where it was, he reclaimed the microphone.

"All right, Hooded Seven," he told his own radio set, "you can relax. It's safe enough, and looks like it'll remain so for some time yet to come. I'll keep a lookout as we talk, just to make sure. It's only a fifteen-year-old kid and a bemmie from some dust-bowl planet, any-way. What are you so frightened of?"

Several heartbeats went by before the voice replied. "*Earthman*"—an undertone of weariness colored the words—"*we, too, have traveled far to meet you in this place. For you, the local environment, while differing in various insignificant details from that which you would regard as most comfortable, is at least somewhat familiar. For us it is extreme, harsh, alien, and dangerous. We would find it taxing to attempt coping with discomfort, disorientation, and the necessities of self-defense, all at the same time.*"

Aha, thought Geanar, the mysterious Hooded Seven reveal one more detail about themselves. He wondered how he could use the information to his advantage.

Aloud, he asked a question. "All right, granted the environmental problems, which I find quite uncomfortable enough, thank you, what do you mean self-defense? Self-defense against what?"

Again a pause of several heartbeats. "*Very well, human, since you insist upon hearing the naked truth: aside from the ever-present dangers represented by savages and the many voracious nonsapient life-forms dwelling within the Sea of Leaves, there happens to be you, yourself.*"

Geanar's jaw dropped, but his expression of wounded innocence was lost over the radio. "Me? Of all people? Listen to me carefully, Hooded Seven, this is strictly a business proposition for me. Value for value, as the materialistic expression would have it: you're going to pay me for something you find more useful than money; I'm going to accept in exchange for something I value a great deal less than your money. Granted, the entire affair's crass and sordid and of no higher spiritual significance whatever, but what conceivable reason would I have to injure or betray you? How could that possibly be in my interest?"

This time the wry amusement was undisguised. *"By your own account, you have injured or attempted to injure many others in pursuit of this business proposition, human. Why should we be exempted? Precisely because you are as alien to us as the environment, we cannot know what your interests may embrace. And there is another, better proven danger."*

"Yes?"

"Not long ago our instruments detected an energy pulse of impressive magnitude. It lingered only for a nanosecond, but its output peaked at five million watts."

Geanar started. "Five million—five megawatts! Why that dirty little sneak thief! Not gone a day and he rifled through my closet and found his father's...ahumm. I begin to see. The source, Hooded Seven, is essentially the same as the radio leakage, and maybe I can do something about it. If that's what's delaying you."

"We are not delayed, human. As we have unmistakably implied, we are on our way and on schedule. Keeping your earlier failure in mind, do as you will about potential interference."

It was Geanar's turn to laugh. "And potential witnesses, as well?"

"As you have said, human, would the presence of witnesses be in your interest?"

Geanar shook his head, another gesture which the radio was incapable of conveying. "No, and there you've a point—that it wouldn't. Nor, I suppose, would it be in your interest, considering all the trouble you've taken to conceal yourselves and the fact of your existence from the Galactic Confederacy."

"We are not entirely unknown to others, human, only to those whose potential for interfering with our interests we have not yet been able to assess. In the meantime, we suggest, for optimal mutual satisfaction, that you leave us to look to those interests, and we will leave you to look to your own. Is this agreeable?"

153

Geanar grinned, this time fully aware his emotions were un-known to his listener. "Indeed it is, Hooded Seven, indeed it is. Both agreeable, I'd say, and inevitable."

"Far be it from us to disillusion you in that regard, human, but we feel obligated to point out that we—and our motivations—must surely be as alien and incomprehensible to you as you and yours are to us. But enough of this for now. Do whatever you think best about the presence of other parties at our meeting ground. When we speak again, it will be, as the saying goes, face-to-face."

"I shall," Geanar replied, feeling a sudden chill again and wondering why, "be looking forward to it."

Chapter XIX:

An Illuminating Experience

An early, overcast darkness had begun to descend over the Sea of Leaves, and even at the modest speed of which it was capable, the *Compassionate* had disappeared over the horizon when Middle C found Mac and Pemot trying to relax in their little camp.

For Mac, the vegetation beneath his moss-shoed feet had an uneasy feeling of anticipation, as if something dwelling deep within it were somehow restless tonight. Given that Pemot's inflatable sandsled represented the only solid footing he could place between himself and six miles of unknown horror that stopped only at the bedrock core of the planet, it wasn't a comforting thought.

The taflak had departed a short time after the persuasive display he'd put on for the captain-mother, for another of his hunting trips and to scout around. Somehow, the Majestan had understood both of his alien friends would soon be hungry, and with the weather closing in it was important to move. In almost no time, he'd returned with a fat brace of Parthian-transplanted sea-fed hare.

Mac didn't care.

He'd found his opportunity to hide behind a bush—not difficult when the entire planet was made up of bushes—and, as a result, hadn't felt quite so comfortable and contented in a long time. He was going to have to do something about his malfunctioning suit, however, and given the level of technology the lamviin seemed to operate on, he was hesitant to ask Pemot for help.

155

While Middle C skinned and gutted his kill, a process much neater and quicker than the boy had ever imagined it could be, and started one of his minuscule and almost flameless camp fires, less easy than it looked as a scattering of raindrops began to fall all about them, the lamviin had resumed fiddling with his radio receiving gear again, taking elaborate care to keep it covered and dry.

"Well," he asserted, removing the earphones from his knee joint for a moment, "I believe we've now empirically established that neither the Antimacassarites nor the Securitasians are the source of those signals which I recorded earlier."

"Oh yeah?"

His other physical needs attended to, Mac had wandered nearer the lamviin, the sled, and the taflak's fire where the brace of spitted hare had begun sizzling, beginning to have some interest in food after all. Somewhere far away on the horizon an enormous and dazzling bolt of lightning leaped from the clouds, now a solid purple-black overhead, into the Sea of Leaves.

A loud crackle issued from Pemot's earphones, audible even where Mac stood. Mac counted a slow twenty-five before he heard a distant growl of thunder, and found himself hoping it had zapped Captain-Mother b'Tehla right in her bustle.

"Good thing you weren't wearing those contraptions. How have we established that?"

Pemot attempted to wipe moisture from his carapace with a reflexive, almost uncontrollable shudder, much the same way a human being might react to finding a large, hairy spider crawling up the back of his neck. When it rained in the Fodduan capital city of Mathas, perhaps once every dozen Sodde Lydfan years—a fine, almost invisible mist adding up to a full hundredth of a lamviin finger's-width of precipitation—all traffic stopped, businesses and schools shut down for the duration, and uneducated peasants, trembling and fearful, who still believed water was a poisonous acid which would eat straight through their exoskeletons into their brains, muttered prayers to Almighty Pah.

They were sometimes joined in this by scientists, scholars, and college professors.

Trembling and fearful.

156

"In the first place," the lamviin answered, "because I'm receiving the elusive and mysterious carrier wave this minute—or would be, if I dared put these contraptions, as you call them, back on—which would be a handsome feat for the *Intimidator* to accomplish. In the second, because it appears to come from a different direction than the *Compassionate*. And in the third, because out of fear of being detected by the loathsome and dreaded Confederacy, no Antimacassarite commander would tolerate a radio set aboard her vehicle."

"If you believe the captain-mother." Mac watched with concealed amusement as his Sodde Lydfan friend seemed to twitch with every raindrop that struck his fur. The boy's own hair wasn't even damp.

"If you believe the captain-mother," Pemot agreed. "One of the few emotions I trust absolutely to translate one to one among sapients, be they human beings, lamviin, taflak, or what have you, is good old-fashioned paranoia. Speaking of which, would you kindly hand me that tarpaulin? At an intellectual level I know better, but this downpour's beginning to threaten my sanity."

Mac laughed, reached for a folded sheet of transparent plastic tucked into one of the bundles on the sand-sled, unfolded it, and draped it over the lamviin, tucking the corners in beneath the six feet he happened to be standing on.

Captain-Mother b'Tehla had a great paranoia, all right," the boy suggested, "between her fear of the Confederacy's influence and her bigoted distaste for the taflak."

"Ha, ha!" Pemot exclaimed without humor, pointing a plastic-draped finger at the boy. "Pair-of-noia: an English pun, no better than the Fodduan variety."

"*Shee no leek taflak?*"

Mac shook his head to clear his ears. "Latin, actually—or maybe Greek. Maybe we could both switch to limericks, instead. And can't we do something constructive about Middle C's vowels, Pemot? Another few days of his dog-whistle accent, and I'll be stone deaf."

"What would you suggest?" asked Pemot. "Just talk, to him, to me. He'll eventually catch on."

He addressed the native. "No, my trusty warrior friend, Captain-Mother b'Tehla doesn't like taflak at all, and now, thanks to you and your spear thrower, she'll like them even less in future, I believe. She respects them, however, which was more than sufficient to our needs at that particular moment. Thank you, indeed, Middle C."

He repeated the native's real name.

Mac tried repeating it after him.

The native cringed and reeled off several paragraphs of high-frequency taflak chatter.

Pemot looked at Mac. "He asks whether he and I can't do something constructive to improve your accent."

The boy had never heard a lamviin giggle before.

Lightning struck again, this time much nearer by.

The lamviin's earphones crackled, thunder answering almost at once.

In a few seconds, rain began falling in a manner which even Mac would have agreed was a downpour.

Something *screamed*.

Before any of the three knew what had happened, the rainy night was filled with a different kind of roaring, as a hurricane seemed to begin to blow. Mac had a brief glimpse of a polished fiberplastic hull blurring by, leaped backward, and was missed by no more than inches when the hovercraft streaked past.

Inside the machine, a man-shaped figure raised a fist and shook it at them.

"*Pemot!* Are you all right?"

The sudden mechanized assault had destroyed their camp fire and dinner with it—the aroma still lingered, even in the rain—plunging them all into darkness.

"Quite." The calm voice issued not a foot from the boy's elbow. "What in the name of Romm was that?"

"I'm not a hundred percent sure." Mac drew his plasma gun as he answered, this time making sure it carried a full charge. "But I believe that was my grandfather."

Lightning flared.

No more than a hundred yards away, the boy could make out the familiar outlines of a popular early-model Preble Trekmaster, turning for another pass at them. It had been covered with some dark, open-meshed fabric and a layering of leaves and branches which were blowing off behind it in the slipstream.

Middle C was nowhere to be seen.

What tracks the Trekmaster had left lay straight across the spot he'd been standing on.

Beneath the steady rolling of thunder and the maniacal hiss of rain, Mac could hear the Doppler-distorted thrumming of high-powered electrostatic impellers, their baritone pitch whining higher and higher up the scale until it reached tenor. Blackness slammed down about them once again, bringing with it dense sheets of cold, hard-driven water. Mac ignored the blue-green dazzle spots before his eyes, and raised his five megawatt Borchert & Graham, pointing the massive, tapered barrel at the last place he'd seen the hovering machine.

"Here he comes again!"

Mac took up trigger slack. His pistol's designator beam sprang into scarlet life, splashing across something other than leaves—much nearer than a hundred yards, now—connecting it in a hard, bright line to the muzzle of Mac's pistol.

Ignoring an important point of marksmanship—for the sake of avoiding the worse consequence of flash blindness—he squeezed the trigger, closing his eyes just beforehand.

Even through his tight-shut eyelids, he could see a ball of sunlike fury roar away into the night. It struck the hovercraft the slightest grazing blow and bounced into the foliage, burning its way down toward the surface of the planet.

As Mac opened his eyes, the first thing he saw was a yellow-white searchlight shaft, striking upward into the murky sky from where the plasma ball had begun tunneling. From somewhere within those violated depths, a horde of small, furry shapes poured up and outward, shoulder to shoulder, spreading across the sodden leaves and disappearing into them again. The hovercraft was spinning around and around like an insane top, still headed for them.

Pemot had begun firing now as well, holding his quaint reciprocating chemical-powered projectile pistol in all three hands, rested on one of the bundles in the sled.

Unnoticed, his protective tarpaulin had slipped off his rounded, shoulderless form.

Oblivious to the rain, which seemed to increase in volume every second he rocked back and forth, hands lifting with the recoil of each shot, keeping up a steady pulsing rhythm of gunfire—his weapon's muzzle flashes were short-lived globes of pale blue-pink in the inky darkness—until the magazine was empty. He ejected it with one hand, replaced it with the other, all the while keeping the gun trained on the vehicle with the third, and recommenced shooting.

Mac closed his eyes and fired again.

And again.

When he opened them, he saw the attacking machine had veered off at last. It still appeared to be out of control, spinning about its axis, but was slowing.

Off to one side, the shaft of plasma light winked out.

That, for the moment, at least, was the last he saw of the car, although he thought he heard it shudder to a stop with a groan of mechanical weariness and injury.

He jumped.

Something small and quick had scurried across his foot.

Beware of the rats.

When the next bolt of lightning illuminated the Sea of Leaves, the damaged hovercraft was nowhere to be seen, although that meant nothing in itself. By now, visibility had been reduced to nothing at all—perhaps six feet, perhaps seven—by what seemed to be a solid wall of water all about them.

Seeing no sensible alternative, they bent and felt the moss for yards around, at last retrieving Pemot's plastic tarpaulin, both amazed it hadn't blown away. The emergency energy of adrenaline—and its lamviin counterpart—had begun draining from their bodies, leaving them limp. Between the intermittent thunder and the steady roar of wind and rain, they were forced to communicate at the tops of their lungs and could still scarcely hear each other.

Fighting storm winds as well as their own fatigue, they draped the plastic over their shivering bodies and huddled together under the inadequate lee of the uptilted Fodduan sand-sled that every moment kept threatening to tear loose from where it had been tied to the vegetation and sail high and free over the distant and invisible horizon in mindless pursuit of the *Compassionate*.

Misery loves company on every planet in the galaxy.

Middle C joined them in their unhappy huddle just before a dawn which, although still wet and windy, was promising to clear. His short pelt was streaming, and his supply of spears—and energy—was exhausted. It was the first time Mac, or even Pemot, had seen a Majestan tired out for more than a moment.

Speaking in dull-minded monosyllables, his own tribe's version of taflak laced with pidgin Fodduan and English, he assured both of his offworld friends he was uninjured, thanks to an inborn reflex which had sent him burrowing into the leaves without a conscious thought, the moment he'd seen the danger coming.

Death, it seemed, had passed directly over him.

He, too, had been trying his best to kill the fusion-powered monster before it killed them.

He, too, had no idea whether they'd succeeded.

And what was worse, he'd brought them more bad news.

Chapter XX:

Tunnel Rats

M iddle C insisted on explaining in his own way.

Dawn had broken over the Sea of Leaves, the sun of Majesty bursting through a ragged covering of clouds, fleeing from the sky as if they'd been caught staying out too late. Birds and birdlike creatures sang. Everywhere the vegetation glistened in the morning sunlight as if it had been edged in silver.

The humidity was ninety-eight percent.

The two offworld travelers, Mac and Pemot, had been too weary the night before to listen to their taflak friend. For his part, he'd maintained that, although they were in terrible trouble—again—it was trouble that would take some time arriving. Although worried, the three had enjoyed total, limp unconsciousness for several hours—Mac was learning the secret of sound sleep: terror and utter exhaustion—awakening to a world transformed from the stygian bedlam of wind and rain it had been to a pastoral symphony of sunshine and birdcalls.

It made Mac nervous.

Middle C made one of his small fires again, although he wouldn't hunt this morning. Instead, they all snacked on the last of Pemot's field rations—even the taflak, with his single supporting tentacle coiled beneath him in a sitting position, nibbled at the dried and salted sandshrimp which were a lamviin delicacy and one of Pemot's personal favorites—boiled tea, and *kood* smoke.

162

At last, when the human and the Sodde Lydfan could stand the suspense no longer, Middle C took up his spear thrower and, with many a high-pitched warble and whistle, showed them both a feature of it which neither had known existed.

"He says," Pemot translated, "that, unlike Earthians and lamviin, who invented pockets because they seem to have convenient places on their anatomy to hang them—" The scientist patted the pockets covering the legs (or arms) of his own trousers (or tunic). It was more than just an illustrative gesture. He'd misplaced his monocle in the previous night's excitement and seemed lost without it. He'd already mourned the passing of his radio equipment which had been reduced to sodden junk. "The taflak, unblessed anatomically, have had to arrive at some alternative arrangement. He directs our attention to the handle end of his spear thrower."

This, it developed, was hollow, friction-sealed with a tapered plug. Thanks to his implant, Mac had followed more of the native's speech than perhaps Pemot suspected. Now he heard Middle C explain the courage and strength which obtaining the materials for a spear thrower required on this vegetation-covered planet.

"*Branches large enough to make spear throwers—and spears themselves—come from deep beneath the Sea of Leaves, the deeper beneath the sea, the larger the branches. A warrior is required to burrow down and cut a branch of the correct shape and size. No one else may do it for him. It is one of the rites of adulthood.*"

"I'd wondered," Mac confessed. "There doesn't seem to be anything large enough on the surface."

Pemot blinked. "Yes. I gather it's also the source of the finer stems and branches their village platforms and dwellings are fashioned from, as well; although such materials as these must come from shallow enough depths practically any villager can—"

"*Queet so!*" Middle C answered Pemot's guess in English and continued in his own language.

"*If he has won a large enough thrower, a taflak warrior carries his few possession here...*" The native pulled the tapered plug from the end of his spear thrower, splayed the dozens of hairlike tendrils at the end of one tentacle, and allowed the contents of the hollow handle to spill out onto the "palm" he'd formed.

163

Everything Mac saw had been made in miniature: a spool of some sort of thread or twine, a couple of spare spear tips which could be used as knives, a bundle of herbs, fire-making tools, several items, including some small, hand-polished wooden washers or doughnuts, which neither he nor Pemot could identify.

And a foil-covered roll of candy.

The kind with the holes in the middle.

"This, I take it, is why you say you've bad news for us this morning, Middle C?"

If the native nodded, winked, or gave any other nonverbal sign in the affirmative, it was lost on Mac.

"*Every gathering bag contains at least one decaying berry which, if left alone, may spoil the rest.*"

"Which means?" Mac asked.

"*Most taflak, even those you have disagreements with, are fine people, if you get to know them well enough. All they want is good hunting, a dry, safe place to live, a happy mating, and perhaps, if they are ambitious, a better life for their offspring.*"

Middle C indicated the wooden doughnuts. "*For dealing with such people, I carry these. They are tokens for which food or metal can be traded.*"

"Good heavens!" Pemot exclaimed. "A monetary system which I didn't even dream existed!"

"*But for others,*" Middle C continued, "*the decaying berries in the gathering bag, I carry this.*"

He held up the spear thrower itself, and, thought Mac, would have indicated the spears if he hadn't spent them all on the hovercraft last night.

"*You New Strangers are much the same,*" stated the native. "*You carry metal tokens for good people, and, for the decaying berries in your own bag, you carry death spewers.*"

He laid a gentle tentacle first on the holstered reciprocating pistol attached to Pemot's upper leg, then on the Borchert & Graham plasma gun at Mac's side.

"I see what you're getting at, old fellow." Pemot blinked understanding. "But what—"

"*It is not comfortable to tell you, although I must, that some entire tribes among the taflak have become decaying berries. Mostly tribes in the*" *barren lands. They trade with the Old Strangers, exchanging their will-ingness to do evil for crazy coins.*" Now Middle C held up the roll of perforated candies.

Pemot answered, "Hmm."

"I get it," Mac offered. "New Strangers—us Confederates. Old Strangers are the First Wavers. Some tribes near the poles do their dirty work, for candy?"

"Why," Pemot asked Middle C, "do you call them crazy coins?"

"Because, slipped around the end of one's tentacle, they dissolve slowly, and make you do crazy things."

Mac shook his head. "Candy's a drug for the taflak?"

"It would appear so," answered the lamviin. "And where, might I ask, did you acquire this?"

Middle C took the roll of candy and, rising, threw it as hard as he could out into the Sea of Leaves.

"After we fought the death machine, I scouted around. Polar tribes are coming this way, following the slave machines of the many wheeled tribe of Old Strangers. I sneaked into their encampment, listened to them talk, and took this to show you. They would travel much faster on their own, and we would be dead by now, except that they do their masters' bidding and come at their masters' pace."

"So," Mac translated, "the bad news is that more Securitasians are on the way, backed up by hostile tribes."

"Hostile drug-crazed tribes," Pemot corrected.

"Yes," affirmed Middle C, *"that's part of the bad news."*

"Only part?" Mac and Pemot had spoken at the same time.

"Yes, they travel slowly because they are afraid. Many whirly machines of the other Old Strangers also come this way."

Mac swallowed. "Why do I have a feeling, Pemot, that this is still only part of the bad news?"

"MacBear is smart. The worst of the bad news is that the many-wheeled Old Strangers, the whirly Old Strangers, and the decaying berries, all of them, come from many different directions."

Middle C raised a tentacle and swept it around in a circle, follow-ing the horizon.

"In short," offered Pemot, "we're surrounded."

"The good news," Middle C chirped, *"is that this is all of the bad news."*

"Well, what can we do about it?"

"I have already done what I can do. These movements cannot go unnoticed by my people. When they discover our plight, they will no doubt come and try to help us."

"Gee, that's confidence-inspiring," Mac observed. "Any ideas of your own, Pemot?"

"Hmm. I seem to have a rather short supply of ideas at the moment. Where do you suppose your grandfather went with that hovercraft of his? Even damaged, it would be a good deal faster than either the taflak or the First Wavers."

"Ha!" Mac answered. "And my grandfather would be real likely to help us out, too. On the other hand, if he's stalled somewhere out here, he's in the same mess we're in, isn't he? And if it meant his own escape—and if he needed us to help repair his machine…"

"Three ifs, MacBear. Nonetheless, they appear to be the only hope left to us."

"Not quite."

"Oh?"

"Yeah. I came here for the Brightsuit. I never intended to leave without it. And now, I may not be able to leave without it. Remember, it's essentially a one-man spaceship, complete with weaponry. If I can get it away from my—"

"Another if, MacBear. I never have more than three with my breakfast. I accept that we need to find your grandfather's hovercraft, for one reason or another. Therefore—"

"You want to go and look for the death machine?"

Mac laughed. "Yeah, as crazy as it seems, we do. Do you know where it is?"

"No, but I do not think it went far, and I should be able to find it easily. Should I do this now?"

"We'd appreciate it greatly—but do have a care, will you? You've none of your throwing spears left. Don't get too close until we're there to back you up."

"Agreed. I have acquired great respect for these death spewers you New Strangers carry. I will avoid any such that may be with the machine and await the protection of your own."

166

While Middle C departed to look for the damaged Trekmaster, Mac and Pemot cleaned up their camp, packed their remaining possessions, and stowed them on the sand-sled. Pemot even found his eyeglass, hanging by its ribbon from a broken radio antenna section. They hadn't been at it ten minutes, when they heard a loud hooting not far away. Looking up, they saw Middle C waving a pair of spears in the air, which he'd recovered from where they'd fallen the night before. He went on with his search as they continued with their camp chores.

The taflak hunter returned in half an hour with news. He'd found the Preble hovercraft upright and intact. Following his agreement with Pemot, he hadn't approached it, but he had a keen eye which had discerned no activity within it.

The pair of outworlders trudged off in the native's impatient wake.

It took them all much longer than the half hour Middle C had required to find the Preble Trekmaster. Long before it was within sight, the warrior halted them, advising them to keep low and maintain silence. Pemot's sled would be left where it was.

From Mac's viewpoint, the area they'd come to was identical to every other spot on the Majestan equator. Flat, for the most part, from horizon to horizon, the Sea of Leaves formed low, rolling features too small to be called hills.

Mac wondered how Middle C could tell one place from another.

That he could soon became evident. Peeking out from behind a "bush"—a lump of vegetation raising itself a few feet above all the other vegetation—they spied the crippled machine lying at a slant amidst the leaves. One side window was cracked. Scorch marks and bullet holes showed where Mac and Pemot had scored hits.

And, visible inside, movement.

Drawing his pistol, the boy started forward, only to feel a three-fingered hand on his shoulder.

"Excuse me, MacBear, just what is it you hope to accomplish this way?"

Irritated, Mac squatted back down and turned to the lamviin. "What we said. Check out the machine. Make a deal with my grandfather. Double-cross him and get the suit back."

Pemot made his throat-clearing noise, and it occurred to Mac for the first time that he must have picked it up from other humans he'd known, perhaps on Earth.

"Is it possible for larceny to run in families? Never mind, in this case I approve the broad outlines of your plan. Nonetheless, it'll most likely get off to a bad start if your grandfather shoots you before you can speak to him."

"You've got a point. What should we do, show a white flag?"

"And provide him with a better target? No, I believe we should confer with our mutual taflak friend instead."

Middle C had been waiting, impatient, for the extra-Majestan council of war to conclude. Hearing Pemot's reference to him, he came closer and asked what was required of him.

"I hesitate," Pemot told him, "to send you into danger on our account, old fellow, but I should like to know if it's possible for you to burrow all the way to the hovercraft under the covering of leaves."

"*I myself burrowed down over fifty body lengths to obtain this, my three-eyed friend, a mere half body length is playtime for children not yet hutbroken.*"

"Very well, we'll either await your signal to follow on the surface or your return to tell us it's unsafe."

"Why not follow him under the leaves?"

"What?"

"*MacBear has a good idea. I burrow, you follow. It should not be more difficult than walking on the surface.*"

"Dear me, I—"

"Claustrophobic, Pemot?"

"Of course not! I'm simply cautions. Very well, for Triarch and Empire, and all that sort of dryrot, let us go forward!"

Middle C began to whirl, not tentacle-over-tentacle as he did when traveling on the surface, but about the axis of the tentacle he was using for a leg. In a twinkling, he sank into the leafy "ground" like a post-hole digger.

Before too many seconds had passed, the taflak had disappeared from sight, leaving a narrow, cylindrical tunnel behind him, perhaps four feet from side to side. For a moment, the noise of his passage—which sounded to Mac something like the ice crusher in Mr. Meep's kitchens—ceased, followed by several chirps and whistles.

"Hurry, my friends, before it can grow closed behind me!"

"He says," Pemot translated, "we must hurry, or—" Mac firmed his grip on the Borchert & Graham. "I heard him. You go first."

Giving the Sodde Lydfan fur ripple which was the equivalent of a human shrug, Pemot drew his own weapon and climbed into the hole which Middle C had left behind him.

For both of the offworlders, it was like crawling through a translucent green plastic tube. This close to the surface—they were never more than inches from it—plenty of light found its way between and through the leaves. Pemot picked his way along, placing each of his six feet with exaggerated care, just as he did on the surface.

Mac's moss-shoes continued to work as they had above. The boy wondered how the vegetation, as green here as above, at this and lower depths got enough light to stay alive.

On occasion he brushed a nervous hand at the unprotected back of his neck or caught Pemot in a similar gesture. Small, gray, many-legged things skittered out of their path before they could quite be seen. Some ran along the ceiling. The leafy walls rustled with the movement of the creatures living within them.

And with something else more sinister.

Mac happened to look back for a moment, and noticed the hole they'd entered by had disappeared—along with several yards of the tunnel they'd just come through.

"Hey! This thing's closing up behind us!"

Pemot's rear eye blinked at the boy, and the lamviin replied without slacking his pace. "Indeed. That's why our trusty guide felt compelled to hurry us. The planet's vegetation's incredibly mobile, churning and turning over like a thick soup boiling in a pot, so all the leaves can be in sunlight for some part of their existence."

He raised a hand to brush at the walls, only to have a rat stick its head out from between the leaves and snap at his fingers, which he was quick to withdraw.

"Ghastly creature."

Pemot reholstered his reciprocator and drew a large, curved, gleaming knife.

The next rat which tried to bite the lamviin lost its head.

"In any event," Pemot went on, "for all we know, these leaves around us now may have begun their lives at the bottom of the sea, a full six miles below us, just last year."

Mac, who didn't have a large fighting knife and hadn't yet learned to reduce the power of his father's plasma gun—if it could be done—used the heavy barrel as a club to kill a rat the size of a small dog which had lunged for his ankle.

Squealing and whistling came from ahead of the lamviin. Middle C was disposing of rats by the tentacle-full, as if they were part of the worldwide hedge he bored through.

"*I have never seen anything like this number of rats,*" whistled the native warrior. "*Something from below must have driven them up out of the leaves.*"

Mac wiped blood and fur from the front sight of his pistol, looked at his hand, and shivered. "What do you think, Pemot? Could it have been the shooting last night, that one wild plasma ball of mine?"

"Or something else," observed the lamviin. "I don't believe that ball went deep enough."

"*Turnover,*" the taflak commented as if he fought for his life every day in this manner, "*goes as deep as where the leaves begin, about thirteen hundred body lengths down. Further below, in the eternal darkness, something which is the essence of ugliness reigns in their place. Perhaps this is what we disturbed, and it disturbed the rats. Be quiet, now, my Stranger friends. It is not ever good to speak of such things, and here and now is a worse place and time than most.*"

Mac looked down between his feet, imagining the black and horror-filled depths below them, and shuddered.

Something warm, furry, and fast-moving dropped onto his smart-suited shoulders.

Heart racing, he seized it and *twisted*, feeling bones crackle before he threw it away.

Sweating all over, Mac ordered his heart to slow. He turned his attention forward, curious about how Middle C was creating the short-lived tunnel they moved through.

The taflak was neither cutting nor boring his way through the vegetation. Instead, as he turned, his forward tentacle insinuated its way between the leaves, stems, and branches, feeling out a path of least resistance, while his pair of trailing tentacles, so quick-moving they blurred into one another, widened the spaces by tucking, almost weaving or braiding, the vegetation away into the walls.

On Earth—and on Sodde Lydfe, the boy guessed—such an arrangement would have been permanent. Here, it took the plants a few minutes to untangle themselves and resume their earlier position, or another which couldn't be told apart from it.

Even some of the rats Middle C had braided into the vegetation would be able to return to their old, wild ways, as he didn't take time to kill most of them.

Each in his own peculiar way, Middle C turning like an auger, Pemot tiptoeing on six three-toed feet, Mac shuffling along on his moss-shoes, the three trudged onward.

Dozens of hard-fought yards and hundreds of dead—or, at the least, inconvenienced—rats later, they came at long last to the dark at the end of the tunnel.

They were beneath the shadow of the hovercraft.

Chapter XXI:

Well-Chosen Words

Burrowing up through the covering of leaves while Middle C and Mac did their best to keep the rats from bothering him, Pemot raised an arm and thrust a sensitized smartsuit finger up over the bullet-riddled fuselage of the inert machine.

He yanked it back down.

"Here's where all our rats are coming from, gentlebeings."

The lamviin whispered, rolling his large eyes upward, toward the hovercraft, as he did so. "They're flattened against the windows. The thing's jammed to the scuppers with them!"

In the comical squeak which served his species as a whisper, Middle C wanted to know how Pemot could say that without—apparently—looking. Also, what scuppers were.

Keeping his own voice low, Mac explained the various optical capabilities of smartsuits, which could be programmed to look like weather-beaten jeans or any other kind of clothing. The more accomplished and expensive models could also receive light on any portion of their surfaces and retransmit it to the inside of the hood, which Pemot had pulled up over his eyes before surveying the car.

Mac also confessed he didn't know what scuppers were, annoyed that an alien should have a better command of the English language than he, a native speaker, had.

"Never mind that," Pemot insisted. "We've got to get those rats cleared out. Any ideas?"

Middle C admitted he had none.

"Unfortunately, I do," Mac offered, hesitating, "but I sure don't like it much."

He told them what it was.

They didn't like it much, either, but, lacking weapons appropriate for dealing with hundreds, perhaps thousands, of voracious rats—Pemot's pistol would do until he ran out of ammunition, Mac's was too powerful, Middle C's spears were the best they had, but even he admitted they were inadequate—it was the only idea they had.

This time, when Pemot stuck a rubberized finger up through the leaves, it was from beneath the machine. This one, although it was an electrostatic impeller model without fans or other moving parts, was an early example of its kind. It still retained the deep, skirted plenum cavity and wide-mouthed topside intake funnel of a propellor-powered hovercraft, for much the same reason many automobiles continued to look like carriages much longer than they had to.

The cavity was deserted: nothing down here to eat, Pemot theorized, and nothing else to interest the rats. The three companions climbed and burrowed back toward the surface of the leaves, taking care to be as quiet as they could about it.

Sifting in through the translucent hull, the light beneath the disabled machine was dim and filtered, like that of a shaded greenhouse. It was so hot inside—or damp—even the lamviin had trouble breathing. Pointing upward, toward the metallic mesh which would have been a coarse air filter on a propellored hovercraft, but which, in this one, constituted the primary lifting mechanism, Mac got a boost from Pemot, seized the woven wires above his head, and began cutting through them with the lamviin's saw-backed survival knife, assisted from below—the boy had to be watchful to keep both thumbs—by Middle C, the lamviin, and the taflak's pair of long-bladed spears.

In a few moments, the mesh had been opened, and they were standing on top of the machine.

"All together now!" Pemot's voice was no longer soft. "One, two, *three!*"

He and Mac and Middle C began jumping up and down on the battle-scorched body of the car, screaming as loud as they could and banging on it with whatever implements they had. The hovercraft bounced on its resilient skirt, sinking a trifle deeper into the leaves. A dark, furry, squeaking torrent issued from the broken windows, vibrating the machine as the thousands—or, as it seemed to Mac, millions—of rats it was composed of jostled one another where the frame constricted the flow, and leaving a thick, rich, nauseating smell in its wake.

Mac's eyes watered. He coughed and went on jumping, landing hard on both heels, firing his plasma gun into the air, burst upon burst. Even in full daylight the five megawatt flash was dazzling, and he felt deafened by its sharp-edged roar.

Pemot's eyes watered. He sneezed through all six nostrils and continued jumping, as well—six feet to Mac's two—banging on the already dented roof as he did so with the butt end of the spear he'd borrowed from Middle C.

Middle C's eye turned a slight yellow, but, although he only had one leg to jump with, he followed Pemot's example, relying on his other spear and the end of his spear thrower to contribute to the terrifying racket they were trying to make.

They went on with the performance until they were all three hoarse and exhausted, the hovercraft had sunk to its scuppers—whatever they might be—in the Sea of Leaves, and what they hoped was the last rat had squeaked with indignation at its tormentors, lashed its pink and naked tail, and abandoned the damaged car.

Mac sat down on the roof of the Trekmaster, elbows on his knees, trying to catch his breath. Refilling its reservoir, he kept his Borchert & Graham handy against the return of the rats, having decided "too much gun" was a contradiction in terms.

Pemot and the taflak rested as well, but as the minutes passed and they regained strength, they recalled more trouble was on the way and their time was limited.

This time it was Middle C who preceded them into harm's way—they seemed, with no particular design in mind, to be taking turns at it—both razor-edged spears poised. Pemot followed with the taflak's thrower raised like a club.

Mac followed the lamviin with a pistol in each hand, hoping he wouldn't have to use either one. "Too much gun" or not, he realized his own would be about as useful in an enclosed space as an atomic

174

flyswatter, and Pemot's seemed to have been constructed upside down, to fit his peculiar three-fingered hand.

The Sodde Lydfan, having an appendage to spare, turned the recessed metal T-handle in one of the Trekmaster's gull-wing doors and waited a moment with the panel open a few inches for any lingering rodents to depart. When none took the opportunity, he lifted the door the rest of the way and let Middle C pass by.

The Preble Trekmaster was a fair-sized hovercraft, intended for rough country and bad weather, the Confederate equivalent of an ancient four-wheel Rover or Landcruiser. Between the doors lay a cargo area behind the passenger seats, with a flat floor like one of the antique English taxicabs which sometimes carried tourists around one shopping deck of the *Tom Edison Maru*, or the back of a small truck. Although the taflak and the lamviin weren't cramped, Mac, the tallest of the three, didn't have quite enough space to stand up in.

Inside the hovercraft, everything edible—by rat standards, which meant everything softer than aluminum—had been stripped out by the gnawing teeth of the thousands of rodents which they'd driven away. The floor carpet had been eaten down to perforated chrome-magnesium and fiberglass. The wall fabric and headliner had vanished. Even the four seats were no more than skeletons of steel.

And on one of them sat a skeleton of bone.

"MacBear..." Pemot's voice was as gentle as he could make it. "Was this your grandfather?"

Mac looked across the seat backs at the skeleton.

It was clean and polished. Here and there a tooth-mark showed where the rats had been trying to get to the marrow. No doubt they'd been interrupted by the noise on the roof. Still held together by their drying tendons, the bones looked like a schoolroom demonstration model. Nothing whatever remained to identify them.

"I don't know." The boy's answer wavered, his stomach feeling uncertain. "I—hold on, what's this?"

He leaned forward and picked up the tattered spine of a hard-backed book. Nothing was left of the pages, but the rats hadn't cared for the plastic cover.

"*The Confession of Frater Jimmy-Earl*. It's my grandfather, all right—Dalmeon Geanar."

175

Inside himself, Mac wondered, not for the first time, why he couldn't feel anything: love, hate, sadness, glee. It was as if all of this were happening to someone else, someone—

"Hey! Where's his smartsuit? Has it been eaten? Do you suppose they got to the Brightsuit?"

In the same instant, Mac felt guilty for thinking about anything but his grandfather, who'd died a horrible death. He shook his head. What else should he have been thinking about? Dalmeon Geanar had been a criminal, at least twice a murderer, and had gotten everything he deserved. He—Mac—had come here to rectify one of the old man's crimes, and this was all that mattered.

Middle C reached out with a spear butt and tapped the side of a long crate lying between the front and rear seats. Preoccupied with the remains of his grandfather, Mac hadn't noticed it before. It, too, had been gnawed and nibbled around the corners and along the edges but was otherwise intact. Perhaps it had been impregnated with some repellant or preservative when it had been warehoused by Laporte Paratronics, Ltd., or even at A. Hamilton Spoonbender's museum.

It was, in absolute fact and without a doubt, the same crate he'd seen the workmen take out of their plant-filled Lindsay Arms apartment aboard the *Tom Edison Maru*.

Padlocked cables had been wrapped around the crate the last time Mac had seen it. They were gone, now, although he doubted the rats had eaten them. The seams of the container looked as though they'd been sonic welded. Mac borrowed one of Middle C's spears and set to work, trying to pry one end open. He was soon joined by the curious taflak, but Pemot declined when invited to take part.

"If I recall aright, MacBear, the man fancied himself a religious being, did he not?"

Worried more about the Brightsuit and the safety of the immediate neighborhood—those rats wouldn't stay away forever—than Pemot's memory, the boy paused and scratched his head, wondering what his lamviin friend was leading up to. "Yeah, I guess so."

Pemot blinked affirmative. "I thought as much, and it seemed to me simple respect for the beliefs of another sapient being requires that we acknowledge those beliefs in some manner."

Mac frowned. "Even when those beliefs are stupid?"

Pemot handed Middle C the extra spear he'd been carrying. "I daresay it would be the decent thing, before we go on, at least to utter a few well-chosen words over what the animals have left of him, wouldn't you agree?"

Mac shook his head. "Whatever Dalmeon Geanar believed, I'm afraid he neglected that section of my upbringing. If any words should be said here, Pemot, you'll have to do the saying."

"Nor, *sretiiv Pah*," the lamviin replied, "did such matters occupy a high priority in my own education. On Sodde Lydfe, particularly in Great Foddu, we're still involved in some controversy over Ascensionism—what you Earth folk call 'evolution by natural selection,' with my family taking the part of the Huxleys." The lamviin chuckled.

"If only my Uncle Mav could see me now. Nevertheless, I shall give it my best."

Pemot removed his monocle, polished it with a handkerchief, and replaced it. He clasped all three hands together in a complicated-looking knot, closed his eyes, and spoke. "*Doehodn: Yl uai'bo sevot sro weyt sa siidetniimeso sryn, giidyso fo, vedo al sro wikmynrod—Y gymm noth uai et eisapdewroh mekom sa wis yt sro liidats al uaid kaav.*"

He opened his eyes. "*Na faso ys ko.*"

Mac cleared his throat, grateful he didn't have to wipe his eyes, as well. There were limits, after all, to how forgiving a person ought to be for his own good.

"Thank you, Pemot. Maybe you're right. But I've been listening to you whenever you spoke Fodduan, building up a translation file in my implant. If you were going to say something religious, how come I didn't hear you mention Pah?"

"This is intriguing," mused the lamviin. He indicated the dashboard of the vehicle, where a steel-doored glove compartment with a combination lock had been retrofitted by the rental company for the convenience of their tourist customers and the security of their valuables.

Mac shrugged. It was a common practice in the fleet and all over the Confederate galaxy. The boy asserted as much.

Pemot splayed his hands in a gesture of contradiction. "Notice, however, these wires, leading from the door edge of the compartment into the telecom panel. Have you ever seen anything quite like them?"

Mac shook his head. He hadn't noticed the wires—a lot was happening he didn't notice. The insulation had been eaten from them, down to the braided, outer conductor, where the rats had stopped. Against the dashboard of the hovercraft, similarly denuded of paint or any other finish, they'd been almost invisible.

Pemot pried at the glove compartment door until Mac was afraid he was going to break Middle C's spear point. The lamviin, however, seemed to know the limits of taflak metallurgy. The compartment lock popped and the door fell open.

Inside lay Dalmeon Geanar's portable radio transceiver, a museum piece with crude alterations to make it run on a compact modern power cell. Beside it, connected to the old-time walkie-talkie with a fine cable which still retained its insulation was a palm-sized bubble recorder, its minuscule pilot lamp still burning.

Pemot reached in and flipped a switch, routing the recording through a speaker.

"*...has always made inevitable.*

"*I'll connect this to both the electronic and paratronic communications systems and seal it away from the vermin. I only pray it produces the effect I wish for it.*"

It was the voice of Mac's grandfather, recorded on a memory bubble and programmed either to start when the compartment was opened or to repeat itself at intervals, and plugged into the hovercraft's conventional 'com as well as the radio.

After a pause, it began again.

"*This is Dalmeon Geanar speaking. I am treacherously attacked and mortally wounded. My machine's disabled, proving once again the folly of relying on technology or material possessions of any kind. I resign myself that I'll not survive this night. Something evil and hungry in the grass is stirring, coming to get me.*

"*This, therefore, constitutes my last will and testament.*

"*To any sapient being within hearing of these signals, including the Hooded Seven, for whom I feel nothing but contempt, I leave the Brightsuit, here aboard this vehicle with me now. Whoever wins the fight to keep it can have it, and welcome to it. It's worth its weight or more in precious metals, a fitting token of that self-destructive insanity which compels men to throw away their spiritual well-being in the pursuit of profane knowledge and illusory progress.*

"I only regret I'll not witness the hideous carnage which will result from this broadcast. Those of you who suffer in it will know I've had my revenge.

"To the grandson who betrayed me, Berdan Geanar Bear, if he lives, I leave all the other worldly goods remaining to me, knowing full well that, like his grandmother, father, and mother before him, he's already been corrupted by a preoccupation with the trivialities of the mundane universe, and that, by my last act, perhaps I can hasten the undoing which his bad blood has always made inevitable.

"I'll connect this to both the electronic and paratronic communications systems and seal it away from the vermin. I only pray it produces the effect I wish for it."

Pemot shut the recorder off before it could start again. He reached for the dashboard panel. "Well, at least we've half a chance now of summoning help. Since this vehicle's paratronic telecom served Geanar's purposes, it should—good heavens!"

Sparks flew from the 'com as missing insulation, eaten away by the rats, allowed the device to short and burn.

"So much for that idea," Mac told him, "and so much for summoning help. Too bad they pulled the 'com gear out of the Brightsuit, but they did, and that's that." Mac shook his head.

"Well, I guess there's no need to ask where all our trouble's coming from anymore. Surely the First Wavers have telecommunicators somewhere, of some kind. In any case, the word's out. Too bad about your radio, too. We might've had an earlier warning."

Without bothering to turn around, the trilaterally-symmetrical being reversed his steps, heading away from the skeleton and the rat-stripped seats toward the door, where he peered out of the wrecked hovercraft, back toward his sand-sled.

The boy followed him with his eyes.

"Pah is an ancient Sodde Lydfan god." Pemot gazed across the Sea of Leaves. Somewhere out there, they knew, more enemies were on the way. "Originally a primitive deity named for the sun—or

179

perhaps the other way around, I'm not altogether certain—in any case, a simple, unassuming sun god, although the practice of worshipping Pah has become more sophisticated and abstracted over the centuries. Your grandfather, on the other hand, was an Earthian, concentrated upon different abstractions. The distinction may not mean a great deal to you, but these things matter to some individuals."

"They sure do." Mac's tone was grim. "On Earth, people used to torture and kill each other over matters like that. Maybe you were wrong after all, Pemot, wasting 'a few well-chosen words' over somebody whose final efforts were spent on an act of calculated hate. It's all so dumb. He went to all that trouble, all those years, just to end up here, like this!"

Pemot sighed. "Perhaps you're right, MacBear. If so, I plead temporary humanity. People used to torture and kill each other on my planet, as well. It's one of my fondest hopes, with the coming of the Confederacy, that those days are behind us."

With an exoskeleton, it shouldn't have been visible, but Pemot seemed to take a deep breath, brace himself and turn—in fact, he didn't do that, either—back into the hovercraft.

"Now, hand me your spear again, if you will, Middle C. Let's attend to getting the crate open. Perhaps our salvation lies with its contents. If not, then perhaps, damaged as it is, we should attempt to repair this much-abused machine."

Chapter XXII:

The Confederate Air Force

"That's got it!" Mac exclaimed.

With a final squeal of protest, the top of the crate yielded to Middle C's spear point. As the taflak stood back out of the way, the human and the lamviin seized the other end of the container and slid its contents out onto the floor of the hovercraft.

"My word!" Pemot ran a finger over the surface of the suit, refusing to believe his eyes.

Mac, too, had trouble taking in what he was seeing. The cast, chrome-plated replica back at Spoonbender's had been nothing but the crudest approximation. Even if the Brightsuit had turned out to be the failure everyone had thought it was for so long, it was the most beautiful failure he'd ever seen.

In outline, of course, it was humanlike, from the smooth, featureless oval of the head, down the well-formed chest and back, the narrow hips and legs, to the integral and graceful boots which formed the feet. Not a single wrinkle or protrusion marred its unbroken lines, not even the dual operating keypads which were a customary adornment on the forearms of the ordinary smartsuit.

"It's like a medieval suit of armor rendered in Swedish Modern." Pemot breathed.

Mac, who'd never heard of Swedish Modern, and whose idea of the Middle Ages was somewhat vague, based on dramatic programs about Robin Hood, Ivanhoe, and King Arthur, frowned at the verbal intrusion. The thing before him was too lovely for words.

Even Middle C was speechless, leaning closer on his single leg, humming wordlessly and tunelessly as he examined his own curve-distorted reflection.

Some remnant of the Brightsuit's titanic energy must have augmented what they all saw. No mirror had ever been made which could produce a clearer, more flawless image. It was as if the finish on the surface was spring water, fathoms deep. Whatever else the three companions noticed, it occurred to each of them that, despite all of its rough handling, its many years of storage and neglect, the Brightsuit didn't show the slightest sign of wear or of accumulated grime: not a dent, not a scratch, not so much as a dust speck or a fingerprint.

At last, Mac had to touch it. To his surprise, it was as flexible as any smartsuit, perhaps even more so. Beneath his fingers, which left no print behind when he lifted them, it felt like sheer silk covering warm human flesh.

The wreckage of the hovercraft rocked with the force of a nearby explosion.

Another explosion thundered, even closer this time. The noise was excruciating.

Leaving the Brightsuit, Mac and his companions rushed to the open gull-wing door. From the north-east, they saw the Antimacassarite vehicle A.L.N. *Compassionate* bearing down upon them, its twin screws turning as fast as the slaves could be driven around the threads. As they ran, flames spurted from the weapons along the flying forecastle, threatening to roast anyone who got in the vehicle's path.

What was worse, tumbling cylindrical projectiles were rising in high-topped arcs from launchers on the quarterdeck, falling to one side or the other of the *Compassionate*, and burying themselves deep in the moss where they exploded, showering vegetation and metal fragments back up in a wide-mouthed, deadly funnel.

"Depth charges!" Mac pounded on the lamviin's carapace. "I've watched enough old submarine movies to recognize depth charges when I see them! They must be trying to stop somebody from boarding! Maybe Middle C's people!"

Oblivious to the punishment being inflicted on him by his friend, Pemot blinked. "Wasted effort, for the most part, observe—" The xenopraxeologist was pointing a finger westward, where they could just make out the taflak warrior's tribesbeings locked in combat with their own kind—villagers working for the First Wavers. A lot of screaming and shouting was being done, to the tune of high-pitched hoots and whistles. Thrower-launched spears were flying everywhere. Middle C's people, outnumbered at least ten to one, were being driven backward toward the hovercraft Mac and Pemot occupied.

"*I cannot,*" stated Middle C, taking up his thrower and reclaiming his other spear from Mac, "*with honor permit my tribespeople to perish without perishing myself. I look for you after the battle, here, or in eternal darkness at the bottom of the Sea of Leaves where all of Majesty's dead must go in the end.*"

With this, he leaped out the door, clearing the hull of the Trekmaster, and cartwheeled away.

"I say, cheerful fellow, isn't he?"

Ignoring Pemot's remark, Mac had stripped off his pistol belt and his beaten-up old smartsuit, seized the Brightsuit and begun looking and feeling for the entry seams.

"I don't know how this is going to work out—the darn thing's way too big for me."

Pemot blinked. Having lived on Earth among human beings he wasn't unfamiliar with their naked appearance, but until now he'd always believed them to be as shy about displaying their unprotected bodies as his own people were.

In any other circumstances, he'd have gotten out his notebook and begun scribbling. "By all means, MacBear, try it anyway. We certainly haven't anything to lose now."

Meanwhile, Mac had found the seams. "You can say that again— hey! Pemot, it's shrinking around my legs! It's making itself fit!"

The lamviin gave his equivalent of a shrug. "I don't suppose they call them smartsuits for nothing. Here, get your left arm in here, and consider yourself lucky not to have nine limbs to deal with, squeezing into this suit. Getting dressed always seems to take me forever."

Mac smoothed the front seam in place. He took the flexible hood in his hands, where, like all smartsuit hoods in proper repair, it lay hanging across his chest.

"Well, Pemot, here goes!" He lifted the hood over his face, sealed it at the back of his head, and took an experimental breath. The air collected and processed by the surface of the suit was clean, cool, and dry. The inside surface of the garment began cleansing the boy's skin, treating minor cuts, bruises, and abrasions he'd been accumulating, killing microorganisms, adjusting his metabolism to conditions in which the human race hadn't evolved and couldn't adjust to by themselves. It was the first time he'd been comfortable since coming to Majesty.

"But I still can't—oh yes I can! Pemot, all I had to do was think about being able to see, and suddenly I could!"

"Certainly," the lamviin replied, "your cerebrocortical implant detected the desire and transmitted it to the Brightsuit as a command. Your old suit must have been in terrible condition, MacBear, as this feature is nothing at all revolutionary, any more than is the fact we can hear one another perfectly, although separated by near-perfect insulation. However, I'd be careful, young friend, with this new suit. Considering its alleged capabilities, such a response to your wish could be a dangerous thing, indeed."

"I will be, Pemot."

He stood up, an eerie, mirror-surfaced mannikin, an animated chromium statue. If anything, the Brightsuit's reflectivity had increased since Mac had put it on.

He stepped to the door. "Now I'm looking out over the Sea of Leaves, toward the *Compassionate*. I just thought of being able to see better, and the Brightsuit's optics zoomed right in. Leftenant Commander Goldberry's out on the quarterdeck, supervising the depth bombing—and I've got a notation in glowing letters at the bottom edge of my field of view: five percent ultraviolet has been integrated into the picture."

Pemot had pulled his own hood up.

"Presumably to cut through atmospheric moisture. Another perfectly conventional smartsuit feature. I'm seeing much the same view. Try the Securitasian ship."

"It isn't very different from the *Intimidator*, except for some weird, complicated structure running along the—Pemot! It's a catapult of some kind! One of the overseers is just lighting up the payload basket, a big ball of fire!"

"My word, you're seeing more detail than I am. Is it pointed at the *Compassionate* or at us?"

"What do you think? If they get us, they can divvy up what they get for the Brightsuit, which they can't hurt by roasting us alive. Uh oh, the captain's got a lanyard in his hand. He's sighting along the beam toward us, and—"

"*MacBear!*" Pemot's startled shout followed Mac's reflexive leap into the air, upward and forward, toward the Securitasian vehicle. He met the fireball at the top of its ballistic arc, and batted it with both hands. It fell almost straight backward, along its former course, missing the individuals who'd launched it by a few dozen yards.

Ordinary smartsuits do not fly.

Hanging in the air, Mac—no less surprised than Pemot when the suit had translated this unconscious wish into action—looked down on the Sea of Leaves. The danger they were in was worse than either of them had guessed. He could see several other vehicles coming now, characteristic of both nation-states.

Uncoordinated as they may have been, they formed a solid ring of death around Dalmeon Geanar's ruined hovercraft and the off-world travelers who'd discovered it. But something else was happening as well, something vaster and more ominous. Inside the deadly circle formed by the enemy vehicles, not a thousand yards from the spot where Pemot stood, the Sea of Leaves appeared to be boiling.

The moss churned and rippled with the force of something coming up from beneath it.

Something enormous and powerful.

It was at this point Mac noticed he'd left his Borchert & Graham behind in the hovercraft.

He was distracted by a puff of smoke from aboard the *A.L.N. Compassionate*. Polished, helpless-looking target in the sky that he appeared, he'd begun to draw enemy gunfire. Without his prompting, a hair-fine beam of brilliance, blinding even through his hood, leaped out from the Brightsuit near the back of his hand. Another puff blossomed in mid-air as it vaporized the rising bullet.

This first shot was followed by a ragged and spontaneous volley. Each bullet was converted to plasma hundreds of feet away from its intended destination. Mac watched with amplified vision as Leftenant Commander MacRame shouted at the rifle squad, lined them up, and commanded them to make their fire simultaneous.

A dozen beams flashed out to counteract the Leftenant Commander's military discipline.

Mac was just as surprised when—perhaps because he'd thought of how exposed and conspicuous he was, perhaps because the Brightsuit was reaching the limit of its bullet-destroying capacities—he was whisked upward several hundred yards. At the same time, the surface of the Brightsuit was transformed from perfect reflectivity, to a perfect match for the pure blue of the sky.

Down on the surface of the sea, it must have looked to everyone as if he'd vanished.

He thought about rising higher. Microscopic tachyon lasers in the skin of the suit flared and his wishes were obeyed. Rendered inertialess by the fields it generated, the Brightsuit carried him further into the air every fraction of a second.

Mac scanned the world below.

There's gotta *be someone around somewhere who can help us!*

But he was wrong.

The lamviin scientist, his Sodde Lydfan sand-sled, Dalmeon Geanar's wrecked Preble Trekmaster, the Securitasian and Antimacassarite vehicles grew smaller until they were no more than indistinguishable dots. Even the broad, churning storm of tentacles, spears, and huge, gleaming eyes which were the contending tribes of taflak dwindled to the tiniest of smudges on the face of the Sea of Leaves.

Mac continued gaining altitude.

The sky darkened, blue to purple to black.

Above him, stars winked into sudden visibility, burning bright and steady overhead.

The boy even thought he could discern the curvature of the planet's surface.

At the bottom edge of his field of view, inside the Brightsuit's hood, an amber warning light appeared, indicating the absence of breathable air about him. This was no problem inside the suit's protective and replenishing envelope, but still no sight presented itself, horizon to horizon, of a Confederate presence, no hovercraft, no high-tech equivalent of the tribal rafts used by the natives.

At last, Mac flexed his mind, ordering the Brightsuit to keep him where he was. Hanging at the edge of space, he looked down at the planet. Straight beneath his dangling feet was the equator, where Pemot might be minutes, even seconds, away from death. Somewhere in *that* direction, lay the north pole of Majesty and the settlement of Geislinger. Somewhere in the opposite direction, at the south pole, was Talisman. Both were invisible, far below the horizon at this altitude.

A peculiar surge of pressure ran up his spine.

He realized the Brightsuit had "overheard" his thoughts and begun rising again to some altitude from which he might see the poles. He stopped it where the sky was even blacker than before. The stars seemed like hard, cold chips of diamond.

What should he do now? Where should he go? All he knew for certain was that his friends, Pemot and Middle C, needed help, and none was to be found within thousands of miles. He'd help them himself.

Firming his will, he ordered the Brightsuit to take him down. As friction with the thickening air heated the outside surface of the suit, it began to throw off excess energy in the form of radiation in the visible spectrum.

Inside, the temperature remained constant.

At last, glowing much too bright to be looked at, he swooped like a bird of prey to meet the foe.

The first to feel his wrath was the *Compassionate,* just a few yards from collision with the ruined Trekmaster—where Pemot stood, pistol braced and ready, just inside the door—and already spewing uniformed and moss-shoed rifle bearers. A brilliant beam from each wrist of the Brightsuit traced fiery lines along the *Compassionate's* bow and quarterdeck, splitting the vessel into ponderous, reeling halves which wandered away from one another, spilling slaves who tumbled off into the leaves.

With another gesture Mac drew a line of flame between the hovercraft and the advancing troops. One or two foolish enough to surge onward, despite his warning, exploded like popcorn kernels at the touch of a blinding wire-fine beam.

The rest halted and threw down their weapons, which sank into the sea like stones in pond water.

A Securitasian crankapillar three times the size of the *Intimidator* launched a pair of fireballs straight at the helpless hovercraft. Fire met fire as Mac's energy beams turned the flaming spheres into puffs of harmless smoke.

He beamed down the crankapillar's deck officers, and the machine slowed to a halt.

Last of all, he turned his attention to the battle between the rival taflak tribes. This wasn't quite as easy as fighting First Wavers. In the first place, he couldn't tell one side from another. True, they'd slowed their fighting to watch the spectacle he was creating. Also, he could pick out Middle C waving at him from the middle of the turmoil. But how could he stop it?

"People of the Sea of Leaves!" His shout, rendered in the best taflak he knew, was amplified a million-fold by the Brightsuit. *"Stop fighting and go home!"*

And, to Mac's enormous relief, they obeyed him, splitting into several groups and drifting—from his viewpoint, high above; from their own they were fleeing for their lives (he was gratified to see they took time to rescue most of the floundering Antimacassarite galley slaves who, otherwise, might have perished)—away.

All but one.

Mac swooped down toward Middle C, just in time to see him jumping up and down and gesturing toward the hovercraft. Mac turned in mid-air and watched in horror as the sea surface bulged upward an obscene ten, twenty, fifty, a hundred feet, carrying the Trekmaster and its remaining living passenger aloft with it. Pemot had both guns out, his Sodde Lydfan reciprocator and Mac's plasma pistol, firing slow, heavy slugs and five megawatt bolts of fury into the rising surface.

Mac streaked toward the machine, dived for the door, seized his lamviin friend, and swooped away, splashing whatever lay beneath the vehicle with his brightest, strongest energy beams. Whatever it was became obscured by orange and yellow flames and by thick coils of black, greasy smoke from the burning vegetation, but it subsided, sinking, taking the hovercraft with it into the depths.

When it had gone, nothing but a shallow, smoldering, conical depression remained.

And even this had soon begun to fill in, softened and eradicated by the restless Sea of Leaves.

Chapter XXIII:

Ruby Slippers

The hovercraft, this time an almost-new Blackmon Santa Fe forty-seater, slowed to a side-slipping stop where the world-covering moss thinned at last to bare soil at the border of the human settled polar territory. It sighed as its impellers wound down and its flexible skirt deflated, lowering itself to the ground.

An attendant steered a set of stairs—itself a modified hovercraft—toward the machine's broad, transparent, curving boarding hatch. Mac and Pemot, having offered their good-byes to the passengers and crew, started down the steep flight of metal stairs.

Mac had flown three quarters of the way to the pole to find this excursion machine, had astonished its passengers and crew by alighting on its deck, and, once he'd secured their promise to come rescue Pemot—"superlysanders" had seemed to be the magic word—had flown back again to keep his friend company and to bid farewell to Middle C and the other taflak villagers.

When the hovercraft had arrived, he and Pemot had hidden, snickering behind their hands, as the natives threw the machine's captain and owner into the village cooking pot.

Many of the galley slaves the taflak had picked up, to everyone's surprise (including the slaves', themselves), after being subjected to the cannibal joke, had discovered they liked being free—and uneaten. Others, like Leftenant Commander Goldberry MacRame, with her hair hanging down in limp strings and her sopping uniform already beginning to shrink, hadn't been amused at all.

"I say," the lamviin told his friend, "it would appear we've a substantial greeting party."

Pemot was right. Waiting at the bottom of the long ladder was a small crowd of well-wishers, all of them waving and yelling at the tops of their voices. The first individual Mac recognized, from his tall, battered plug hat and the eternal dark aroma of his pipe, already wafting up the staircase, was A. Hamilton Spoonbender.

Impatient, the man bounded up the stairs to seize Mac's hand. "You did it, Berdan, my boy! Blast me, I never really believed you would, but you did it!"

Mac was forced to clamp his teeth together to keep from chipping them and biting his tongue until the museum owner was through jerking his arm back and forth. Feeling shy, he grinned, discovering he didn't know what to say. "I, uh…"

"Let's get down on terra firma—and believe me, the more firma, the less terra—the whole gang's here to see you, boy, custom delivered by a chauffeured private starship. Everybody, including—"

"Who's your handsome sidekick, Berdan?"

This from the female lamviin, Miss Nredmoto *Ommot* Uaitiip who, as the three reached ground level at long last, seemed to be looking Pemot over with more than casual interest.

"I, madame," replied the scientist, "am Epots Dinnomm *Pemot*, at your service and pleased to meet you. Our mutual friend now travels under the name MacDougall Bear."

"Likewise, I'm sure. Whatever he's calling himself, a lot of high-powered talent's waiting to see him."

Mac blinked, but it wasn't the equivalent of a nod. "What do you mean, Ommot?"

"Well, aside from Hum Kenn, here, Rob-Allen Mustache, Vulnavia, and the kids, there's—"

A hand shot from above the freenie's eyestalk and between the chimpanzee and Mrs. Spoonbender. "Freeman K. Bertram, young man, the chauffeur Mr. Spoonbender mentioned, also President of Laporte Paratronics, Earth. At your service and happy as a clam to see you—not to mention the Brightsuit, wherever you've got it stowed."

191

Bertram was a neat, bearded individual in an expensive business-model smartsuit. Behind him was a tall, well-shaped blonde who somehow seemed familiar to the boy.

"Well," Mac answered, surprised to be able to get a word in edge-wise, "you'll have to talk to Mr. Spoonbender about the suit. It's his. I got it back for him."

The Brightsuit wasn't far away. Much to Pemot's dismay, Mac was looking more like his old self. He'd programmed the Brightsuit to disguise itself as an ordinary, well-worn smartsuit adjusted to look like a sports shirt and Levis. Even at three hundred miles per hour, it had taken the hovercraft over twenty hours to race from the equator to the pole, and the boy hadn't wanted to take chances.

He'd reclaimed his pistol belt and the Borchert & Graham, no longer too much gun for him, although, given the powers of the Brightsuit, it had hardly seemed necessary to carry it on the way back as anything other than additional camouflage.

"Correction, young soldier of fortune," Spoonbender told him. "The suit's Mr. Bertram's—and by right of invention, as well as community property, Professor Thorens'. It belonged to them to begin with. Your parents were testing it for their company. But they've recompensed us handsomely for our claim in it."

If A. Hamilton Spoonbender called it "handsomely," it must have been handsome, indeed.

"You mean," Mac asked, wide-eyed and open-mouthed, "*the* Professor *Deejay* Thorens?"

Spoonbender turned to Bertram and grinned a toothy grin. He turned back to the boy. "Don't let me down. Be sure you hold them up piratically, Ber—Mac, for they're well and truly desperate, I assure you, and can certainly afford it."

Bertram looked exasperated. "Thanks a lot, Spoonbender." The businessman shrugged and grinned. "But what the dirty dishes. You brought it back to us, didn't you, Mac—or should I say Mr. Bear? I knew your dad and mom. Let me tell you, they'd be proud of you today. Why, that's his Borchert & Graham you're wearing, isn't it?"

Mac didn't hear the question, he was busy feeling what he was supposed to, when he was supposed to, and wiping tears out of his eyes as a consequence.

"I don't understand this," he answered at last. "You and your—Professor Thorens—you don't owe me anything. It's still your suit. My grandfa—Dalmeon Geanar stole it to sell to the Hooded Seven, whoever they are, and I got it back for you because of my folks. And because I was ashamed."

With enormous effort, he stifled a sob. Instead, he turned his back to regain control of himself, and, without warning, felt a soft, warm hand on the back of his neck.

"What are you doing to this boy, Freeman?" The voice was soft and warm, as well.

"Dora Jayne, my dear, this is no mere boy you're fondling, but a man in every sense of the word, just returned triumphant from the savage jungle! And by the way, since you're a married woman, I'll thank you to stop fondling him."

"Oh, Freeman, you're so cute when you're jealous!"

Mac turned and gazed into the bottomless azure eyes of the galaxy's most famous—and most beautiful—physicist.

The business arrangements with Laporte Paratronics were simple and straightforward. Mac had recovered the suit, for which Bertram and Thorens felt he was owed a fee. In addition, because the suit had been sold for scrap and later—a legal technicality determined by the timing of his grandfather's death—"abandoned" on the surface of Majesty, it was his by right of salvage.

What surprised the boy most of all was that, even after he'd been recompensed—both handsomely and piratically—he was encouraged to keep the Brightsuit.

"This is the age of spray-painting, boy!" A. Hamilton Spoonbender lectured him. The man seemed to have assumed a kind of spiritual—or financial—guardianship over him which he wasn't certain he liked or needed.

"The computer programs have all been lined up since the first suit was built. All they have to do is push the ENTER button, and *zoot*—a brand-new Brightsuit!"

Deejay Thorens nodded. "We do retain all of the original plans and programming, Mac. We'd also like to borrow your suit for a while, just to be sure what figures Dalmeon Geanar altered and which he didn't. But the fact is, now that it's been thoroughly tested—of course we'll want the readouts—we don't really need the prototype anymore, and you might as well keep it, since it's yours, anyway."

Behind her, Freeman K. Bertram nodded his agreement, beamed, and grumbled as a matter of form.

Mac was stunned. He'd worn nothing but secondhand and hand-me-downs all of his life. Now he owned the newest kind of smartsuit in existence. And he was, at least by his own standards, rich.

The reception party began to drift back toward the hovercraft terminal with eating and drinking in mind. Even here at the pole, the sun beat down hot on the rubberized parking apron. Mac and Pemot, left to themselves for a moment, took up the conversation they'd been having aboard the Blackmon before the settlement had been sighted.

"What I'll never understand is why Geanar didn't use the suit during our battle with him, or afterward, to treat his injuries or save himself from the rats."

Pemot's fur indicated a shrug, followed by a shiver. It had been too cold for his peace of mind, even on the equator.

"I hesitate to point out that the man was your grandfather, Mac-Bear, and that, if you can't answer a question like that, I certainly can't be expected to."

Mac laughed. "You're a big help. Okay, let me see: he knew the suit worked. It wasn't the dangerous failure he made everybody think it was. But what was it to him? A valuable commodity, something to be stolen and sold, like a bag of money, or a—"

"Or a fur coat," Pemot suggested. "I doubt whether many mink thieves try on every coat they steal."

"Vehicle thieves surely do," argued Mac. "People who steal hovercraft or spaceships have to drive away what they've stolen. But to grandfa—Geanar, I mean, the Brightsuit wasn't the vehicle it is in fact, but a suit of clothes."

Pemot blinked. "And so, he adopted the fur thief's attitude, rather than the hovercraft thief's?"

"Yeah, I guess that's the closest we'll ever get to understanding what happened—unless we just say he was a self-made loser and leave it at that."

The lamviin blinked again. "Well I'm glad you were the one to say it, MacBear. I should have been reluctant to do so."

Mac grinned, reached down a hand, and patted the distinguished xenopraxeologist on his furry carapace. It was a stroke of fortune that Pemot had been fully suited up when Mac had grabbed him off the Trekmaster. They'd later learned that close proximity to the Brightsuit in full-powered flight could cause severe tachyon burns.

"I can understand that."

"And," Pemot observed, "I suppose we'll leave the mystery of the Hooded Seven for another time. It was quite clever of them, hiding beneath the leaves in a spaceship."

Mac chuckled. "If that's what it was. I'll bet they were pretty disappointed at what they found in the Trekmaster. I don't know whether I did them any harm, and I don't care. I've had quite enough adventure for a while, my lamviin friend. Not forever, but for now I'm going home. I imagine Mr. Meep'll be glad to see me—as a regular paying customer, rather than a clumsy busboy and apprentice cook."

He lifted an arm, indicating a crowd boarding another of the big sightseeing hovercraft, newcomers to the planet Majesty of all sizes, shapes, and species. Gorillas, orangutans, and chimpanzees kept company with smartsuited porpoises in implant-directed wheeled frames, and even a little human girl and her dog.

"Maybe it's up to somebody else to solve the mystery."

Pemot blinked. "Perhaps it is at that."